A PERFECT
COMBINATION

CHERYL BARTON

Published by:
Barton Publishing, LLC

This book is a work of fiction. Any references or similarities to actual events, real people, living or dead, or to real places, are intended to give the novel a sense of reality. Any similarities in names, characters, places and incidents is entirely coincidental.

Barton Publishing, LLC
P.O. Box 962
Reisterstown, Maryland 21136
www.bartonpublishingLLC.com

Ordering Information:
Quantity sales. Special discounts are available on quantity purchases by corporations, associations, and others. For details, contact the publisher at the address above.

Orders by U.S. trade bookstores and wholesalers. Please contact publisher@bartonpublishingLLC.com

ISBN: 0615922937
ISBN-13: 978-0615922935

Dear Reader,

2013 has been an incredible year for me. I spent the year doing so many firsts, the main being writing my first romance novel, ***Bachelor Not For Sale***, sharing with you, Duron Knight and Taija Charles' rocky road to love. I'm grateful for everyone who has supported this novel and I hope you have been enjoying my walk forward, fulfilling a dream. I never thought that I'd write my first novel and that I would get such great feedback on what started out as a class assignment. From the moment the first novel was released, I realized there would be no stopping me. While finishing up that first one, I had dreams of a follow-up story which turned out to be ***A Designed Affair***, bringing you the love story of Michael Bailey and Loren Knight. Now here we are with ***A Perfect Combination***, a second follow-up story about an unexpected, but perfect love for Tyrone Davis and Victoria Alston.

I'm hoping that my vision for novels in 2014 will keep you entertained and will have you falling in love with my characters again, and again, and again.

Thank you,
Cheryl Barton

ACKNOWLEDGMENT

Thank you to my daughter, Chynae, for being my number one supporter. You encourage me daily to never stop writing because I was meant to do this.

I do all that I do because of you. I love you!
Mommy

Prologue

Michael Bailey was packing up the office in his, soon to be wife, Loren's condo to have more of her things shipped to California where they now lived, when his phone rang. It was his friend and business partner Tyrone Davis. Mike assumed Tyrone was calling about the conference he was attending to represent their company, Pioneer Architecture & Design, in Houston, Texas.

"Hey Ty. What's up man?"

"Not much. The conference is going well. I was asked to present tomorrow about modern structures. I'm looking forward to that. Say listen, a quick question. Do you remember the name of Taija's friend that came from Boston to be in her wedding?"

Mike had to think for a minute.

"I don't know. Let me ask Loren."

Tyrone waited as Mike checked with Loren.

"Her name is Victoria Alston. Why what's up?"

"I think I saw her at the conference today. At least I think it was her or it was someone who looked just like her. I'll say hello later if I run into her again and see if it's her.

If so, she looks good. I remember how fine she was when she was in town for the wedding. I may have tried to hook up with her if that girl I brought to the wedding didn't act like a second skin. I got rid of her right after that. I should have known better than to take a date to a wedding. What was I thinking?"

Mike laughed at his friend. He remembered those days. He happily gave them up for the current love of his life and wouldn't change a thing.

"Go for it man. Hope that works out for you. Don't forget Taija's baby shower is in two weeks and then my wedding next month. Don't bring any unwanted, clingy guests."

"Yeah, I hear you man. One day I'll learn. Until then, I'll hold down the single brother's club since you and Duron bailed on me. I guess it's just me against a world of beautiful, willing women and I certainly don't want to disappoint them. Give Loren a kiss for me and I'll see guys when I get back."

"Later man," Mike said, shaking his head at Tyrone. He knew that Tyrone wouldn't be singing that happy singles tune if he had found a woman like Loren. When he does, Mike dreaded the day Tyrone found the one. He couldn't imagine what all the single women of the world would do if Tyrone was off the market too.

~~

Tyrone was about to head back into one of the breakout session rooms when he spotted the woman he thought was Taija's friend, Victoria. She was just as beautiful as he remembered her being at the wedding. Tyrone ventured in her direction to see if it was her and to say hello.

"Excuse me, but is your name Victoria Alston by any

chance?"

"Yes it is," she replied.

"I thought that was you. My name is Tyrone. I'm best friends with Taija's husband Duron. I met you when you came to Atlanta to be in Taija's wedding."

Victoria could never forget him. She knew exactly who he was. She remembered him from the wedding and how sexy he looked in his all black tuxedo.

"I remember you, Tyrone. Nice to see you again. What are you doing here?"

"I'm speaking at the conference this week on modern design structure. What about you?"

"I work for a major financial corporation that deals with financing major construction projects and we are one of the vendors for the week."

Tyrone thought of how good his luck was.

"Since we are both here for this last night of the conference, would you join me for dinner later? We could dine right here at one of the restaurants in the hotel."

Victoria was not going to pass up the chance to sit across from this fine specimen of a man.

"I would love to."

She checked her watch and realized she needed to get to her last session of the day.

"I need to get into this last session. What time would you like for me to meet you?"

"Why don't we meet in the main lobby at eight o'clock? I'll make reservations at one of the restaurants, if that's okay with you."

"That's fine for me. I'll see you at eight Tyrone."

Victoria turned to head in the direction of her last session and smiled at the prospects of spending the evening with such a handsome man.

'Whew, what a man,' she silently said to herself.

~~

Tyrone watched Victoria walk away and couldn't help but notice her long, toned legs. He realized she had a magnificent pair. It just happens that his favorite part of a woman was her legs. Nicely toned, sculpted legs were a major turn on for him. He could imagine what hers would look like wrapped around his back as he entered her body over and over again while gripping on to her toned legs. He needed to clear his head and get to his own final session of the day. There would be time for elicit thoughts later on at dinner.

~~

Tyrone woke the next morning feeling great after a long night of sex with the most extraordinary woman he had ever met. After dinner he and Victoria could barely keep their hands off of each other as they made their way to his room. The rest of the night was a blur. He remembered enjoying the hottest sex of his life and he wanted more. He was glad he was waking up early. One more round of sex would be great. Besides, he loved early morning sex before starting his day.

He turned to reach for the very naked Victoria only to discover the other side of the bed empty. He sat up and looked around for signs of her and realized she had left. He didn't see any of her clothes that were strewn around the room haphazardly from the night before when they couldn't wait to undress each other and get to the sheets. He got up to look around his suite, checking to see if she was in the bathroom. He looked, but no sign of her there. He went to the outer sitting area and again, no sign of

Victoria. He was stunned that she would leave without even a goodbye after the night they had spent sexing each other every way possible known to man in the few hours they shared. He was hoping to see her again before she left. He had one more day at the conference, but he knew that she was leaving today because her last session was the day before. Tyrone decided to try and catch her before she left to find out why she dashed out on him. He called the receptionist desk to have them ring her room.

"Yes hello, this is Tyrone Davis. Can you ring room four twenty eight for me please, the room for Ms. Victoria Alston?"

"I'm sorry sir, but Ms. Alston has already checked out."

He wasn't happy with that information. It's quite obvious to him that Victoria wasn't happy about the events of the night before and was expecting to avoid it all together by leaving before he woke up. He smiled to himself. He knew for a fact that she couldn't avoid him forever. They would see each other again. A lot sooner than she thought. He knew for a fact that he would be seeing her at Taija's baby shower and he would ask her why she felt the need to leave like a thief in the night. The least she could have done was to leave the money on the night stand.

Tyrone moved about his room to prepare for his day knowing that he looked forward to seeing Victoria again and he had plans to make sure the one night they spent tasting each other would not be the one and only night.

'Be afraid Victoria. Be very afraid. I'm going to give you a little space, but not much. Now that I've had a taste, I want more of a meal,' Tyrone said to no one in particular.

Chapter 1

"Can I get you anything to drink?" the airline attendant asked Victoria.

"Just some water," she replied.

She smiled as she accepted the water while on a plane back to Boston after a very eventful trip to Texas. Victoria quickly gulped the cup of water, needing the cool relief. All thoughts of the night before made her body tingle and heat up. Her mind was so occupied with the events of the night before that she barely heard the sound of the crying baby in the row behind her and she wasn't annoyed as she usually was. The man who occupied the seat next to her talked nonstop since they'd taken off, but she couldn't remember anything he spoke of. Mayhem could break out around her and she wouldn't notice. As much as she tried, she couldn't get thoughts of the night she'd spent with Tyrone Davis out of her head and the way she felt the need to twitch in her seat let her know that her body remembered him too.

She'd never been with a man before who consumed her thoughts like Tyrone was doing right now, after only spending one night with him. Thoughts of him even now caused her to twitch in her seat, to try and find a way to get some relief from the sudden rush of want her body was experiencing, remembering what it felt like to feel him as he did things to her body that she'd only dreamed about.

She wasn't a virgin or new to being with a man, but being with Tyrone was brand new for her. She had never been as uninhibited as she had been with him and she was shocked at her own behavior. If he hadn't made her feel so sexy and racy, she would have been embarrassed.

Victoria turned to see if anyone could see that she was becoming flushed. She hoped it wasn't noticeable to anyone but herself.

She'd wanted to wake up in the morning and experience more of what she'd had the night before, but pure exhaustion from the activities of the night before had completely drained her. By the time she'd awakened, she didn't have much time before she needed to get checked out of the hotel so that she could make her flight back to Boston on time.

Tyrone looked like a sexy devil as he slept in the bed next to her. She woke to his long, lean body wrapped all around her. She wanted to stay in that cocoon with him intricately woven with her, but time was not on her side. She took great care sliding from within his embrace and out of the bed without waking him.

Victoria watched him as she looked around the room for her clothing, strewn everywhere. She remembered how they wasted no time getting each other undressed and placing clothes neatly was the furthest thing from either of their minds.

They barely waited until they had exited the elevator that led to his room before clothes started flying. She was glad he remembered to go back into the hallway to grab the belt she had removed from his pants while he tried to get the hotel room door opened. After taking it off of him, she dropped it to the floor and proceeded to devour him. If he hadn't shown restraint, she would have dropped to her knees and taken him into her mouth, an act she never performed on a man so soon. It wasn't something she did often with a man, but there was something special about Tyrone that made her want to experience it with him.

She had been pressed against him on the elevator ride up to his room and could feel how long and thick he was. Images of that part of him poised and ready for her attention is what drove her almost to the point of not being able to wait to get in the room before she had him with his pants down around his ankles.

Tyrone struggled with concentrating on getting the door opened, especially with the things she had been doing to him with her tongue. She was in front of him against the door and had somehow gotten his shirt opened. She used her lips and tongue to kiss and lick all over his chest, something that without a doubt he loved, proven by the moans her acts elicited from him. As he fumbled with the key card, trying to reach around her to get them in the room, Victoria had removed even more of his clothing, trying to save time once they did finally get in the room. Victoria didn't want to waste any time getting him inside her body; it was a must.

She didn't know what had come over her. After spending most of the evening over dinner and drinks getting to know Tyrone, she was already picturing him naked from his first hello.

"Looks like we're about to land," the gentleman next to

her said, breaking into her thoughts.

She was glad he'd said something. She needed the reprieve from her thoughts or she was going to have to take matters, literally in her own hands by taking a quick trip to the restroom. Her body craved what it had experienced the night before. She couldn't think straight because all she could think about was the many ways Tyrone had pleased her all night long.

"Yes," she replied as she noticed the 'fasten your seatbelt' sign come on right before the captain announced they were making their approach into Boston.

Victoria couldn't help but wonder what Tyrone was thinking by now because she was sure he was wondering what happened to her when he woke. She'd thought of waking him before she left but she wasn't sure she would have made her flight in time if she had. There was no way she would have left that room without another roll around in the sheets with him. He had looked so heavenly lying in bed, with a look of satisfaction on his handsome face.

She remembered meeting him for the first time at her friend Taija's wedding. He was one of the two men who had served as best man. Her first sight of him had caused her mouth to dry up and her tongue felt like it had stuck out and was wagging like a dog in heat. He was finer than any man she'd ever seen before.

Tyrone was over six feet tall. His look reminded her a little of Tiger Woods and now she knew why.

During the time they'd spent getting to know each other over dinner, he had shared with her his heritage. His mother was Asian and African American and his father was African American with a little Thai in his family line. That accounted for his exotic look, which made him beyond handsome. Tyrone was drop dead gorgeous, as most ladies would say. She should know since it was her first thought as well. He did favor the golf player except that Tyrone had facial hair which consisted of a neatly trimmed moustache and goatee. She loved rubbing her hands over the short waves of his hair, loving the feel of the smooth texture. His waves were so heavily defined and natural, which she assumed was from the combined heritage and the strong presence of his Asian lineage. When he smiled, he lit up the room with a perfect set of pearly whites. He had the body of someone who worked out constantly and she remembers appreciating it very much as she found her way around it all night long with her hands, her tongue and just about any other body part that she could connect with his.

She shook her head like a cartoon character to snap out of her state of arousal thinking about him. She had a life to get back to and she had to let what happened be exactly what it was. It was a one night stand. She didn't regret it. She just knew that she needed to move on and forget about it. She only hoped Tyrone didn't think too bad of her with the way she completely gave herself over to him after sharing an evening of great conversation, dinner and drinks.

She appreciated how he continually asked her how much she had had to drink because he didn't want her judgment to be clouded with what he had planned for them once they'd reached his hotel room. She assured him, she was in complete control of her faculties.

"It was nice talking to you," the man next to her said, once again interrupting her thoughts.

"Yes, it was and good luck with your job interview."

She didn't quite remember much of what he conversed

with her about on the flight, but she did remember him saying something about coming into Boston for a job interview and he was nervous about it. She figured it was why he talked nonstop to keep his mind off of it.

After the plane landed, she grabbed her one carry-on bag from the compartment above her head and made her way through the concourse to grab her luggage. She was sure Turner was already at the airport waiting to pick her up. She decided to put all thoughts of Tyrone Davis behind her as she grabbed her suitcase and turned to see her fiancé Turner Warfield, head in her direction with a purposeful stride. As soon as they saw each other, he lit up like a Christmas tree, as he always did when he saw her. She returned the smile and hoped that she would be able to conceal from him what was really on her mind. Her fiancé was headed her way and her mind was on Tyrone and the sexy night they'd just spent together. She was in dilemma.

Chapter 2

Tyrone walked into his office after taking a few days off to regroup after his business trip to Texas. He had agreed to attend the conference alone so that Mike could stay in California and attend to his fiancé Loren.

Mike was not only one of his best friends, but he was also one third of the partnership in the architectural firm they ran with another of his best friends Duron Knight.

Mike was engaged to Loren Knight, Duron's sister he couldn't be more happy for them considering things could have turned out so differently for them.

It had been a few months since a woman Mike had once been involved with had run Loren down with her car, angry that Mike had fallen in love with Loren, casting her to the side. Tyrone had been just as concerned for Loren as anyone else, even though they were not family. He still considered Loren like a sister to him since Duron was clearly the brother he'd never had. Duron and Mike both were.

He and his two best friends met when they were

students at Howard University in Washington, D.C. The three of them took engineering and architecture classes together. They became instant best friends and never had a doubt that they would one day go into business together. They now ran a very successful architecture and design firm and their business was growing by leaps and bounds daily. It also helped that the three of them were featured on the cover of Black Enterprise Magazine as the three to watch. Since then, business had skyrocketed and they have been able to not only increase their staff, but they were also in the midst of opening up a west coast office to be closer to new projects they were beginning in that area.

From the beginning Tyrone had considered Duron and Mike as brothers, though he had two brothers of his own that he had an unbreakable bond with. Tyrone didn't have any brothers that he knew of and he was lucky to have them.

Now that their business was expanding, they discussed who would do the biggest brunt of the traveling and he immediately agreed especially since lately his two best friends had been focused on their personal lives. Mike wasn't the only one who'd recently given up the single life.

Duron recently married Taija and they were expecting twins. Mike and Loren were getting married soon, having gotten engaged while Loren was being treated in the hospital. During her stay it was discovered that she was pregnant. He was the only single one who had the time to commit to traveling so he volunteered without hesitation to take over a big portion of the work that was out of town. It wasn't that he didn't have any family. He still had his grandmother who lived in Texas where he was from, but that was pretty much it for him except for other extended family members. He didn't even want to give any thought to his estranged mother or his wayward father who he discovered had another family, even while his mother was pregnant with him. He'd never met his father and didn't know his name. He only knew that his father had been married at the time that he was conceived and that he'd had two other children, both girls, but he didn't have any brothers, so his friendship with Duron and Mike meant everything to him.

Tyrone was about to go into Duron's office to give him an update on what occurred in Texas when he looked up to see his best friend walk into his office.

"What's up D? I was about the come see you," he said, getting up to greet his friend with their usual handshake and fist bump.

"No problem. I figured I would stop in here to see you before I headed out."

"Out?" Tyrone asked.

"Taija has a doctor's appointment and I don't want to be late for it. I was late for the last one and she read me the riot. That doctor's office will never be the same again. I'm hoping they'll let her back in."

"Knowing her, I'm sure she let you have it good. Are you coming back in the office today?"

"Yeah, I should be able to make it back later this afternoon. After her appointment, I'm planning to take her for a nice lunch. I thought about taking the day off to spend it with her because I've been so busy this past week, with you in Texas, and Mike back and forth between here and California, but she informed me she had plans with my mom this afternoon so I should be back by two."

"Okay, I'll have everything ready to brief you by the time

you get back. Have you talked to Mike today? What's going on with him?" Tyrone inquired.

"Actually, he's in town. He came in this morning. He'll only be here for a few days I think, and then he's heading back to California. He's around here somewhere. He flew in only because my dad and my brother Brian flew out to check on Loren and he knew she shouldn't be alone."

"Cool, I'll check in with him in a few. I have some phone calls to return first."

"So the trip was a success?" Duron asked, taking a seat in front of Tyrone's desk.

"Major success, man. I won't even tell you about the number of inquiries we received regarding new projects. I gave all of the contact information to my assistant and I've asked her to email everything to you and Mike later on today. There were some pretty big pockets in attendance. I was surprised at how many had already heard of us and had known about some of the projects we'd already completed. I did commit to at least taking a look at some of the proposals and scheduling sit-downs with them to discuss ideas in greater detail. I figured we could then decide what we'd be able to add to our already full plate of projects," Tyrone said.

"Sounds promising, Ty. Great job on the conference. I look forward to the full briefing. Make sure Mike's still going to be here later. If not, let's patch him in via phone. It would be great if we could get it in before he returned to California," Duron said, standing to exit.

"I think we'll be able to do that."

Tyrone's mind briefly drifted to Victoria and the night of mind blowing sex they'd had. He wasn't sure if he should tell Duron about his run-in with Victoria. Duron may ask questions Tyrone wasn't prepared to answer and he didn't want it to be a big deal considering the Duron's wife and Victoria were very good friends. He figured Victoria would probably tell Taija soon and Duron would be approaching him about it anyway so he'd just let it go for now.

"Alright man, I'm running to meet Taija. Hit my cell if I'm needed."

~~

Tyrone was about to return the first of his many phone messages when he looked up to see Mike standing in the doorway of his office. He was exhibiting the same type of smile that Duron had been sporting when he was in Tyrone's office before. It didn't take him long to figure out that they both share that happily in love with a fantastic woman who's about to have my baby and I couldn't be happier, kind of smile.

"Mike, what's up man?"

"Not much," Mike replied.

"What brings you back to Atlanta already and how is Loren doing? Duron mentioned that his father and brother had flown out yesterday to see her."

"I actually had a few ends to wrap up here for Loren for LKnight Designs."

Tyrone knew Loren was the owner of a very successful interior design business which she'd planned to expand to the west coast since they now lived there so that Mike could run the west coast office of their company, Pioneer Architecture & Design.

"I'm overseeing the shipment of a lot of the product from her Atlanta store. She was planning to do it herself when she came in for Taija's baby shower, but I don't want her stressing herself so I flew in early this morning to finish things up. I'm finally done and I'm planning to head back to California tomorrow evening. Overall, Loren is coming along good. You could hardly tell not too long ago she'd been hit by a car. The leg that was very badly damaged has almost healed completely. She's been keeping up with her physical therapy and the baby is doing very well. You know I'm thankful for that because things could have been a lot worse. I could have lost not only Loren, but the baby as well," Mike admitted.

Tyrone remembered that day so well. It turned all of their lives upside down. A woman, desperately in need of counseling and therapy had become obsessed with Mike after he'd stopped seeing her once he'd gotten involved with Loren. The woman had used her car as a weapon and had run down Loren and a group of other people. The woman, Shelly, had let her jealousy and anger consume her so much that she did a spur of the moment, irrational act. Thankfully all of the people injured by her act that day had survived and were making full recoveries and Shelly was also getting the care she needed.

"How was the trip to Texas?" Mike asked.

"Very successful. I was actually going to check with you today to see if you had time to sit in on a meeting I'm having with Duron when he returns from Taija's appointment and I can bring you both up to date at the same time."

"That sounds like a plan," Mike agreed.

"I'll have my assistant block some time on each of our calendars."

"Cool. Listen Ty, remember last week when you called from Texas to ask me about Taija's friend Victoria because you thought you saw her in Texas, was it her?"

Boy was it ever her, Tyrone thought to himself.

"Yeah, it was. She was in town at the same conference. Her company sent her there to represent them as a vendor for the last couple of days of the week-long conference."

Tyrone tried to play it cool even as the memory of being with Victoria filled his mind, making another part of his body fill up as well. He was glad he was sitting behind his desk because his pants started feeling a little snug behind the zipper with the thought of her. He needed to change the subject before Mike inquired about what may have occurred after running into her. He wasn't ready to tell him about it.

"So Mike, how are the wedding plans coming along? I know Loren wanted a very small affair with just family and very close friends. Is that still the case?"

"Yeah, we'll be flying back in for the baby shower in a few weeks. I'm going to fly back to California after that to take care of some work things, but Loren will stay here with her parents until our wedding. She decided to have the wedding at her parent's house. You know how big that house is, especially the area out back where we'll have the ceremony and reception. We're having two tents brought in, one for the ceremony and one for the reception. It's still going to be small like she wants. I think she's just anxious to get the ceremony over with and get back to our life in California. Now that she's getting around a lot better since the accident, she's ready to get her office of LKnight Designs up and running in California. She's also ready to have this baby. I know she has some time to go yet, but she talks to the baby every night. She even has me doing it," he laughed.

"Mike, man I'm just glad everything turned out okay

and that the baby is fine."

"So am I. I don't think I would have survived if Loren and the baby hadn't made it through all that. That was a close call. I'm never taking my time with them for granted. It can all be taken away so quickly."

"I hear that. Let me know if I can help you with anything while you're here."

"All I can think of at the moment is that you, Duron and I need to get fitted for our tuxedos for the wedding. It'll be here before you know it. We could get it done when Loren and I return for the baby shower. I'll get my assistant to schedule an appointment for us," Mike said.

"I'll clear my schedule whenever you're ready."

"Thanks man. I appreciate that. I would have tried to do it on this trip while I'm in town, but it was a last minute decision to turn around and come back to Atlanta so quickly. I thought I would be busy catching up here at the office and with Loren's business affairs that I didn't think we'd be able to squeeze it in. Speaking of being busy, I need to get going. I'll be back for the meeting this afternoon. I saw that it just popped up on my calendar," Mike said glancing at his phone.

"I have a lot to catch up on before the meeting so I'll be here all day."

"Looks like the meeting is at three. I'll be back and ready by then," he said before getting up to head back into his own office.

After Mike left, Tyrone was glad his friend hadn't asked any more questions about his running into Victoria. He would hate to have to lie to him, but he didn't want to tell him all that had occurred. He definitely didn't want to tell him that Victoria had run out on him after a night of the best sex he'd ever experienced and he had experienced plenty. If there was one thing he knew a lot about, it was women and there was never a shortage of them for him. He loved women, but he had no interest in any kind of commitment. He stayed true to his nickname, *Mr. Love'm and Leave'm*, a name he was given back at Howard University.

He, Duron and Mike had made names for themselves back then because of the number of women they had bedded while there. He shouldn't be as concerned about the fact that Victoria left him like a thief in the night, not even leaving a note of goodbye or something saying she at least had a good time. Then again, he didn't need a note that said that. He could tell by the number of orgasms she'd experienced that she'd definitely had a good time. He was a master at satisfying a woman so there was no doubt there. It did bother him that she slipped out without waking him for more of what they'd had throughout the night. He must have been dead to the world from exhaustion to not notice she had gotten up and left.

He couldn't understand why the thought of Victoria disappearing on him bothered him. It was, after all, what he always wanted women to do. He liked for them to help him satisfy his insatiable need for the female body and then leave. She could have at least left a number where he could reach her if for no other reason than for him to know she had returned to Boston okay. Their discussion the night before about having a one night stand held true for her and she did just that.

It was some one night stand, he thought. She had really put something on him. Never in his wildest dreams would he have thought she'd had that in her. She had been wild beyond his imagination. No matter what he threw at her, she threw it right back at him. She met him stroke for stroke and every time his mouth opened, she was right there with her tongue, dueling with his.

Victoria had a beauty that was unmatched with any other woman he had ever been with and there had been many. He had even dated a woman who was once a contestant for the Miss America pageant and she was a knockout. Victoria was that, times ten.

When Tyrone had first lain eyes on her at the hotel, the first thing he noticed about her were her legs because he was a leg man. Whenever he saw an attractive woman, his attention went first to her legs. If her legs excited him, that was a huge plus in his book and Victoria had legs that were made for a man's admiration. They were long and luscious and she had a sexy and powerful walk that was strong, but very feminine. She looked incredible in the gray suit with the skirt that had a slit up the side that gave just a peek of her luscious thighs. He couldn't stop looking at her legs every time she sat and crossed them.

All through their dinner, he couldn't help but wonder what type of underwear she wore, and if she wore any at all. Unlike most men who loved a woman in a thong, Tyrone was okay with that, but his preference was in a lacey, high-cut panty. To him, she looked like the kind of woman who took great time and care in selecting the sexiest underwear and every time she spoke, his mind wandered to what was under that skirt.

He was like a kid in a candy store when they finally began ripping each other's clothes off when they reached his hotel room and he caught a glimpse of black, lacey high-cut panties.

He watched her as she walked back into her conference room and loved the form fitting skirt. It was extremely sexy, but also very business-like for the conference they were attending. Her suit jacket, throughout dinner, had been opened to reveal a crisp white blouse that covered what appeared to be a hefty set of breasts. They weren't too big, but big enough that his mouth watered with the thought of what he would like to do to them. All through dinner he imagined licking all around them until her nipples stood out like hard pebbles.

Most men loved women with long flowing hair, causing many women to subsidize with weaves or wigs. He was glad to see that Victoria liked her natural hair, short and in, what he knew women called, a pixie cut. It was a style Halle Berry had been known to rock, but Victoria wore it better. It fit her perfectly.

Her complexion was a golden brown and the bright red lipstick she wore drew his eyes to them constantly throughout their dinner. She looked like perfection and after talking to her and getting to know so much about who she was, he realized she didn't just look like perfection. She was as close to it as one could get. He had not found that complete package in any other woman before. That was probably why he couldn't get her off of his mind.

Her likability jumped to an unbelievable level when she shared her love for old cars and all things on wheels. He too had a mad passion for cars and bikes. He owned several motorcycles and his car collection was still growing. He loved purchasing cars and having them restored. He had also taken to doing some restoring himself on some of his cars. When he wasn't working, he could be found in one of his garages, laid out under one working on something. He loved getting his hands dirty with the grit and grime that came along with working on cars. He had picked up his love for cars from his grandfather.

Growing up in Texas, he and his grandfather spent countless number of days and nights fixing up cars and his grandmother would chastise them for trudging in the house covered in dirty car oil. Those days began his love affair with anything on wheels and when, during dinner, Victoria mentioned how much she loved old cars, the conversation really got interesting. It was erotic listening to her talk about cars, makes, models and engines. He had never met another woman who loved cars as much as he did. She scored major points with him that night.

On his flight back to Atlanta, he thought about asking Taija for Victoria's number when he returned from Texas, but he knew that would bring about more questions than he was ready to answer.

One thing was for sure, he would be seeing her soon. In a few weeks, she'd be coming to town for Taija's baby shower and perhaps he could get an answer from her of why she slipped out without saying anything. He knew they had agreed to a one night stand, but for the first time in his life, a woman who was to be a one-night stand was having a lasting impact on him. Though he liked her, he didn't like how she was already under his skin after one night. He had participated in a lot of one-night stands before and a lot of the women had gotten clingy and told him they'd felt a connection to him after that one night. He didn't understand how they could feel that way, even after an incredible night of pleasure they both enjoyed, but now he understood.

He'd gotten up the morning after Victoria had left him

in the hotel and even though he'd showered and changed, her scent stayed on him.

He was in trouble, he thought to himself as he shook it off and reached for his office phone to return calls from the many messages he'd received while away on business. He was in big trouble.

Chapter 3

Victoria and Turner were enjoying a nice candlelit dinner in celebration of her success at landing a major contract for her company. She was finally getting the spotlight she'd deserved.

After her friend Taija recommended her for a lucrative position at the company, Victoria had taken the ball and run with it. She had returned from the conference in Texas a week ago, but for some reason she couldn't seem to fully relax. It may be the fact that no matter how hard she tried, memories of her night with Tyrone stayed on her mind. She was uneasy every time his handsome face crossed her mind.

They were enjoying a great dinner at one of her favorite restaurants and she was thankful for the downtime. Work had been stressing her a lot lately and her tryst with Tyrone in Texas was continually pricking at her. Never had any man had such a lasting impression on her. She couldn't seem to shake thoughts of him naked and aroused just for her taking. That was exactly what she had done.

What bothered her more than anything was that her thoughts were not just about the great sex, but also the great conversation they'd had over dinner. He was much more than what was on the outside.

Intelligence was a major turn-on for her and the more they talked over dinner, the more she realized she'd wanted him. She remembered the day riding in the car with Taija when they talked about the three best friends, Mike, Duron and Tyrone, who had graced the cover of a popular business magazine. When she'd gotten her fill looking at them in the magazine and reading about them, the article and the photo were nothing compared to experiencing the real thing. All were handsome and successful, but there was something about Tyrone that reached out to her from the pages of the magazine. It wasn't luck that they'd ended up at the conference together. She saw it more like fate and now that fate was messing with her perfect life.

Talking with Tyrone over dinner was like talking to a friend she'd had for a lifetime. The conversation flowed with an endless number of interesting things to talk about.

Once they were comfortable with each other, it excited her that they were able to openly talk about having a one-night stand since they were both in Texas, away from any prying eyes. She shocked herself when the idea of the one night stand came from her mouth. He somehow brought out the tigress in her and he didn't hesitate to agree that a one night stand was the perfect end to their visit to Texas.

Victoria didn't make it a habit of hopping into bed with men, but this man was irresistible. She had no thoughts of Turner while she sat across the table from Tyrone and imagined him naked, on top of her, under her, next to her, any way she could possibly have him and she was open for all the possibilities. She had never really thought of Turner that way, so dreaming about a naked Tyrone and all that she'd wanted to do to his gorgeous body were on her mind constantly that night, without distraction.

Even now she was sitting across from her fiancé and all she could think about was Tyrone Davis. Still after a week, if she moved her body the right way, she could still feel his hardness inside of her. She still had aches in places she didn't know could ache for so long. It was a magnificent ache that she secretly hoped would never go away.

"Victoria, did you hear what I said?" Turner said, clearly annoyed that she wasn't paying attention.

"No, I'm sorry I didn't hear you. What did you say?" she asked.

"I asked if you wanted another glass of wine. Are you okay? You seem to be a million miles away. What gives?"

No way would she reveal her inner most thoughts, especially when they were focused on a naked Tyrone. She worked hard to check back into the conversation with Turner.

"Oh nothing gives. I'm sorry for being a little distracted. Checking out of the conversation was rude. I was thinking about a work thing, but it's nothing," she lied.

"You're clearly distracted Victoria and it looks like more than work. What is it?"

Victoria knew that her opening to tell Turner what happened in Texas was now or never. She didn't want to have that conversation right now so she decided never instead of now and tried to look like she was fine.

"I told you nothing, Turner. I promise I'm fine. It's just work stuff that has had me busy since my return from Texas and with the work I did acquiring that new contract for the company, their expectation of me is on a whole new level. I'm fine, really," she said, trying to sound reassuring.

"Okay, if you say you're fine then I'll let it go, but this is supposed to be a celebratory night so stop thinking about work and enjoy this break."

Victoria knew she needed to do just that before he starting asking more questions she wasn't ready to answer yet.

"I'm glad you suggested this night out for dinner. I'm going to try and relax and leave thoughts of work back at the office."

Quickly, Turner looked concerned.

"If you have a change of heart about marrying me, I will understand. Is that what's bothering you? Is it this whole wedding thing?" he asked.

She felt terrible and she didn't mean for him to think that she was second guessing her decision. He was one of her best friends and she would do anything for him, including marrying him for money. Not money for her, but money for him.

"Don't be silly Turner. Deciding to marry you isn't bothering me. I'm marrying you because you are one of my best friends in the world and you need my help."

She felt better when she saw a hint of a smile on his face.

"Can you make me a promise?" he asked.

She nodded in agreement.

"Will you tell me if at any time during all of this, you change your mind? I appreciate what you're doing for me and that you'd be giving up a year of your life, but my friendship with you is more important than anything else. I would understand if you decided against it."

She needed to reassure him.

"Turner, it's okay, really it is," she said, reaching across the table to take his hand in hers, letting him know that she was on board.

"Don't worry so much. This will all work out just fine."

She could tell the moment the tension evaporated from the atmosphere.

"Good, so no more checking out from the conversation tonight. We are here to celebrate you and all that you have been achieving lately. I want you to know how proud I am of you. Have you had a chance to tell Taija about any of this yet?"

Victoria took a bite of her food before responding.

"No, but I plan to call her sometime this week to tell her about the wedding so that it won't be a surprise when you show up with me as my fiancé. If no one knows about our friendship, she sure does, so she'll be shocked to hear it at first, but I think after the initial shock, I can convince her that this engagement is genuine. She knows we've been close for many years. She may not see us as a couple at first, but she wouldn't question it."

Turner shook his head in agreement.

"What about your parents? When are you going to tell them?" he asked.

That's a conversation she knew she needed to have as soon as possible. Turner's family would be announcing it publicly soon and she wanted her parents to hear it from her first. She was about to respond when Turner's phone rang. She watched as he excused himself from the table to take the call.

Victoria watched her best friend walk away and wondered for the first time what she was doing. She knew deep down she was helping him out, but on the surface, every time she thought about it, she became apprehensive about her decision.

She and Turner had been friends since their childhood days back in the State of Washington where they both grew up. Turner's family, for centuries owned the biggest vineyards in the country, harvesting grapes that were exported to over thirty countries. His family also owned the largest winery known to this country. Turner had come from big money. It was money that until recently, had been far beyond his reach. He had always had money, but not the kind of money he stood to inherit on his thirty-fifth birthday. It was money that came with a stipulation put in place by his grandfather.

Turner had done a great job turning his inheritance into a profitable marketing business in Boston and he was doing quite well for himself. She knew that it had always been his plan to take over as owner of the winery and the vineyards from his father whenever he was ready to step down. His grandfather wanted to be sure the business always stayed in the Warfield family. To be sure that happened, his grandfather put a provision in his will that Turner would take over control of the company only if he married before his thirty-fifth birthday. He did that so that he would guarantee that Turner wasn't out wasting money and going from bed to bed and woman to woman, careless about living the single life. He wanted Turner to be a family man who was just as dedicated to family as all of the other men in his family.

Victoria knew that Turner loved women, but he didn't have plans to marry. He was focused on building his career and preparing to one day run his family's business. He'd also hoped that his own father would relax that stipulation in the will, allowing him to take over without having to settle down first. He knew that his father and grandfather wanted to be sure the business stayed in the family for many more years to come and they needed to guarantee that by making sure Turner settled down and had many sons to one day work in the business as well as take it over one day, keeping the family business flourishing for even more generations.

Victoria never doubted she would help her friend out when he asked her to marry him for a year so that he could inherit the family business. After that one year, they could divorce and she could go back to her life and he could go forward into his. He knew it was asking a lot of her, but at the time, neither of them were seeing anyone seriously and it would be easy for people to believe their engagement was true since they had been friends since childhood and had always been close. People would naturally assume that they eventually would fall in love and marry.

They had tossed the idea around for some time before finally agreeing to do it. She knew that turner could have asked any number of women, but he trusted none like he trusted her and the feeling was mutual.

She hadn't been in a relationship for some time and at the age of twenty-nine, she had given up on finding her Mr. Right. She had come across many 'Mr. Right Nows' but nothing serious. She wanted someone she could have a deep connection with; someone she would go to bed thinking about at night and wake up with him on her mind every morning. She wanted to blush throughout the day at the thought of him and she wanted that nervous feeling when she knew she would be seeing him. She wanted her body to quiver and melt every time he touched her.

Victoria startled herself. She'd just described her every thought about Tyrone Davis.

It can't be, she thought to herself. There was no way she was feeling this way about a man after one night of incredible, unbridled sex. She was still thinking that when Turner returned to the table.

"Sorry about that. That was my mother and she wanted to know if some reporter had contacted me about the news article they're doing on us for the newspaper announcing our engagement. I told her I had, but I haven't returned her call yet. I'll do it later this week as long as you're sure about this whole wedding thing. I know you said you're okay with it, but I need you to be one hundred percent okay with this. I know you're doing this because we're friends, but I don't want you to do this if there is even a hint of reservation."

Victoria thought about it and she knew that this was her opening to speak up. The moment passed as she smiled.

"I'm sure so no more talk about this. Go ahead and call the reporter back and let them know they're about to be witnesses to the biggest wedding of the century."

She smiled, picked up her drink for a quick toast and pushed any thoughts of anything other than enjoying her evening, out of her mind. It was time to get back to celebrating her.

"Okay, now that we're positively on track, its back to our celebratory dinner. Here's to you," Turner said, not seeing the uncomfortable look on Victoria's face. She decided to focus on enjoying the evening and deal with her thoughts of Tyrone later.

Chapter 4

"So as you can see from all the information I provided, the conference was a major success. The amount of interest in our company is increasing exponentially. My assistant is working next week to coordinate with a few executives who want to come and tour the sites we've done so far in the Atlanta area, including our own office building. The modern structures are drawing a lot of attention."

Tyrone could tell by the look on Duron and Mike's faces that they were in agreement with him. He'd finished briefing them on his trip to Texas and they all agreed they would be able to handle the possible projects.

"This is good news," Duron said.

"I agree," Mike chimed in.

"We'll take a look at the projects we'll be able to handle and plug them into a timeline to see what we're working with," Duron added.

"That sounds like a good plan," Mike added.

Duron and Mike discussed more about the west coast operations as well since they were all in Atlanta and didn't have to have the meeting via conference call or webinar.

Tyrone didn't comment on the discussion and Duron and Mike both noticed that he appeared distracted.

Tyrone hadn't realized he wasn't paying attention until Mike flashed his hands in front of Tyrone's face.

"What?" Tyrone said.

Duron and Mike both laughed.

"Man, what planet were you on just now?" Duron asked.

"I'm good," he said.

"Right, sure you are," Mike added.

"It must be a woman so who is it this time? The hot number I saw leaving your condo a few weeks back doing the walk of shame with her shoes in one hand and her panties in the other?" Duron said, remembering the night he and Taija had spent at the condo after seeing a play in downtown Atlanta.

Tyrone brushed him off.

"I know who it is," Mike said, giving Tyrone a side eye.

"Give it a rest fellas."

"Duron, I think he was thinking about Victoria, Taija's friend," Mike said.

"Wait, what?" Duron said, shocked.

"Ty, you didn't tell Duron you ran into Victoria in Texas at the conference?"

At the mention of her name, Tyrone's imagination got the best of him as visions of Victoria in bed with her luscious thighs wrapped around his back like a death grip as he surged in and out of her pliant body. He was imagining her bouncing up and down on him relentlessly pulling every bit of pleasure from him that she needed. He'd felt a connection to her on a level deeper than just sexual. He'd shot off like a rocket watching her as she freely gave up any reservations about containing the beast within.

"No I didn't tell him."

No one spoke.

"Okay, somebody tell me what's going on here," Duron demanded, looking back and forth between the two of them.

Tyrone looked at Mike knowing he had just opened a can of worms while Mike leaned back further in his chair and smiled like he had just let the cat out of the bag.

"Nothing's going on D. Seriously, nothing," Tyrone said, trying to sound convincing.

"Are you sure about that Ty? I've seen her and she's gorgeous man."

"There's nothing there Mike so lay off. I ran into Taija's friend while in Texas and called Mike because I wasn't sure of her name. He asked Loren, she gave me the name and I asked her when I saw her again if it was her and she said yes. Nothing more and I'm not distracted."

Duron looked back and forth between the two of them sensing something else was going on. He knew his friends better than he knew his brothers and something was definitely going on and he had a sneaky suspicion he knew what it was. He looked to Tyrone for an answer.

"Ty, tell me you didn't," Duron said, concerned that Tyrone may have messed over Victoria who was his wife's friend. He didn't need his wife coming down on him about it, if in fact Tyrone did hook up with her.

Like he and Mike used to have, Duron knew that Tyrone had a reputation with the ladies. He never invested any time or energy on really getting to know a woman beyond the bedroom. The only things of importance to Tyrone that

Duron knew besides his grandmother, the company and their friendship was his many cars and motorcycles. Woman were trophies and there would be hell to pay for Duron with Taija if Tyrone was his usual self with Victoria, hitting her off and not looking back.

"D, seriously, I didn't do anything. Look, can we get off of what's going on in my life because there is nothing there; I saw her and that was it. We spoke, exchanged a few pleasantries then we went our separate ways. I told you it was a busy conference and I spent most of my time, when not presenting, networking with others. There's nothing there fellas so move on."

To try and get them to change the subject, Tyrone looked back down at the report, fake browsing through it hoping it would finally steer the conversation away from Victoria.

"Now, I'm glad you both approve of the connections I was able to make while in Texas, but right now I have to jet. There is a '57 Thunderbird being delivered today and I need to meet the delivery at my house in an hour."

Tyrone got up to leave, not looking at either of his friends, knowing if he did, they would see that he was hiding something.

"You've purchased another car, man?" Duron inquired.

"How many cars can one person own? What's that make number seven?" Mike asked, getting up to leave also.

"Don't sound surprised. I've been into cars and bikes since before we were in school together and that'll never change about me. I'm actually thinking of purchasing the property next door to mine just to build an additional garage. The owners have been renting it for a few years now and I got a call they're looking to sell. I could expand my property and double the size of my garage space."

"I'll have to stop out soon to take a look at the new purchase," Duron said. "Don't forget to add the baby shower to your already exploding calendar. I told you its co-ed and she expects to see you there," he said directing his comment at Tyrone. He already knew Mike was coming because he would be bringing Loren.

"I know and I'll be there. I wouldn't miss celebrating with my soon to be god-son and god-daughter."

He dare not mention that he was especially looking forward to seeing Victoria again. He had no doubt she'd be in attendance and he would make sure she didn't disappear on him again before he had a chance to talk to her. Perhaps she'd even entertain a second one-night stand.

"The wedding is a few weeks right after that so add that too. When you get wrapped up in those cars, you forget everything else that's going on," Mike added.

"Hey, you two act as if I'd forget about the most important events in your lives. I would never do that and I'll be there and on time. For this wedding, I'm no doubt coming dateless. I've learned my lesson from Duron's wedding."

~~

The work week had been a very busy one for Victoria. She had purposely kept herself busy so that she didn't have to focus on calling and lying to her parents and Taija. She hated doing both. In order for things to pan out well for Turner, she knew what she had to do. Soon it would be a very public engagement, considering the kind of money Turner came from. She wanted to be sure her family heard about it from her. She decided to call her family first.

"Hey mom," Victoria said when her mother answered

the phone.

"Vicki!" her mother said with lots of excitement. "Your father and I were just talking about you earlier today. How are you?"

"I'm fine mom. I've been busy with work. Sorry I didn't call earlier in the week because I meant too. Is dad around too?" Victoria asked.

"No, he had to run back to the office for some papers. If you need him, we can patch him in. Is everything okay?"

Victoria was actually glad her dad wasn't in. She wanted to tell her mom first and get her reaction before telling her father.

"Yes, everything is okay. I wanted to talk to you both about something, but I'll start with you first. Turner and I are engaged," she blurted out while holding her breath.

There was silence before her mom finally spoke.

"You and Turner are engaged to do what?" her mother asked, clearly surprised by Victoria's news.

"We are engaged to be married mom. He proposed and I accepted."

More silence.

"Really Vicki? I didn't know you two were seeing each other. When did this happen? I know you've been friends forever."

Victoria had actually expected a little more joy than what she was getting from her mom. This was the same woman who constantly reminded Victoria that she was the only child of theirs who was not married or had any children. All three of her siblings were married and two of them had children.

"Mom, you don't sound happy for me?"

"Vicki, I love you and of course I'm happy for you. You

know I've always wanted you to find a great relationship with the kind of love your father and I have always shared, so yes I'm happy for you. I'm just a little surprised it was Turner."

"Mom, you love Turner. He's always been like a son to you since we were young."

"Victoria, don't talk like you have to convince me. I am very excited for you and yes I love Turner. I'm just happy that you are happy."

Victoria sighed with relief.

"I am happy mom."

"Have you and Turner set a date yet for the wedding?" her mother asked.

"No, we're not going to have a very long engagement though. We don't see the need since we've known each other for so long. Do you want to hear the best news?" Victoria asked.

"There's more? You're not pregnant are you?" her mother exclaimed loudly.

Victoria smiled. Only her mother could ask that so easily.

"No mom, I'm not pregnant. After Turner and I marry, I'll be moving back to Washington. Turner will be taking over the winery and vineyards soon so I'll be close to the family again."

The shout she heard on the other end of the phone left no doubt that her mother was very excited about that.

"Vicki, that makes me happy. Your father will be overjoyed. We miss having you close by and you are missing your nieces and nephew as they grow up. This is great news. First a wedding, then to hear you are coming back this way; you've made my day. Is Turner nearby? I want to congratulate him too," her mother said.

"No mom, he's not, but we'll call you both early next week. He's got a lot going on with work and so do I. We're going to Atlanta soon for Taija's baby shower so we'll talk to you before then. I will call dad back in a little while to tell him so don't say anything yet."

"Right, I almost forgot about that and don't forget to congratulate Taija for me," her mother said.

Victoria knew her mother loved Taija like another daughter.

"I won't forget mom."

"Oh, and I won't say anything to your father when he returns. Does Turner's family know already?"

"Yes, they know."

"I'm going to give his mother a call. We have a wedding to plan," her mother said, excitedly.

Victoria was both happy and sad. She was happy that she could bring such joy to her mother, but a little sad as well that she was lying to her.

"Okay, just wait until after I tell dad. I think his mother is planning a newspaper announcement and I want to be sure the entire family knows first," Victoria said.

"Don't forget to tell your sisters and your brother. Don't let them read about it in the paper," her mother suggested.

"I won't mom. I was planning to tell them right after I told you and dad."

"My baby girl is getting married. I'm so happy for you Victoria. I think I hear your dad pulling up now. Do you want to hold on the phone for him?"

"Sure mom."

Victoria paced nervously hoping she'll get a joy filled response to her news from her father as well.

Chapter 5

Now that her family was aware of her engagement, it was time for Victoria to call and inform Taija. She was ecstatic at the reaction she received from her sisters and her brother who were all jumping for joy for her. She couldn't wait to get Taija's reaction and hoped it would be just as joyous. She needed to get it out of the way now before she and Turner showed up in Atlanta together at Taija's baby shower. She had no doubt that Taija would recognize the rock on her finger.

Her thoughts then trailed to Tyrone and what his reaction will be when he sees her and when it becomes public that she has a fiancé. The fact that she was engaged was the one bit of information she'd failed to share with him when they'd hooked up while she was in Texas. It had been a relief to remove the ring while she was away on business, taking a break from her role of fiancé. She loved the ring and happily played the role with Turner, but she wanted to give herself some space from all the congratulations she knew she'd get when people saw the ring.

When she had run into Tyrone, it never occurred to her to tell him because they were simply having dinner. She was presented with many opportunities to tell him before they were naked and rolling around in the bed, all over the floor, against the wall and even the shower, but she got caught up in the moment and how good he'd made her feel that she didn't want to ruin things with talk of a wedding, a ring or a fiancé.

She trembled remembering the shower as an erotic surge went through her body as her mind centered on Tyrone's gorgeous, naked body and all the things that body had done to her in one night. He had the perfect body, definitely made for lovemaking and at that, he was an expert.

The shower action had made her toes curl as she screamed out his name in pleasure over and over as he entered her body again and again. Thoughts of him bending her over to grip the seat in the shower as he pounded without pause into her from behind, making her feet rise up to her toes from his powerful strokes, invaded her mind. Yeah, he did that and she loved all of it.

She shook off thoughts of that night so that she could stop torturing herself. Until Tyrone, she had not been intimate with a man in quite some time. Until him, she had never been as wild and abandoned when it came to sex and that was due to the fact that he encouraged her to not hold anything back and to get what she wanted and needed from him. She trembled again remembering not only was he a master at dishing out pleasure, but he was on top of his game when it came to bringing out the wildness in a woman. She didn't recognize herself when she thought back to the activities of that night with him.

It was because of the complete package that was Tyrone, that she easily agreed to a one-night stand with him. For that reason, she didn't tell him about the engagement. It was only sex and to him, it was one for the road. She knew that's how most men felt about one night stands. They would keep it between them and no one needed to know. Still she wondered if she was on his mind as much as he was on hers. She thought again and doubted it because she knew that there wasn't a shortage of women to keep Tyrone's mind occupied.

She reached for the phone to call Taija.

"Hey Tai," Victoria said when she answered.

"Hey Victoria, I'm so glad to hear from you. You're still coming for the shower right?" Taija asked.

"Of course I'm still coming. I wouldn't miss it and you know it. How are the babies coming along? Everything okay with them?"

She was excited that Taija had asked her to be godmother to the twins.

"Yes, these kiddies are doing great. I'm trying my best to keep them in until the due date. For now everything is checking out good. I'm just ready to meet them," Taija added.

"I know girl, so am I. Have you and Duron picked out names yet?"

"No, he wants to wait until they're born to give them names when we see them. Of course, I wanted to name my little man Duron, Jr. but Duron said he wants the baby to have his own name and his own identity, so no junior. As long as they are healthy, the names don't matter to me.

What's been going on with you? We haven't talked in a minute."

Now was a good time to spring her news on Taija.

"Well, a lot actually. Taija, I got engaged."

"What!" Taija exclaimed. "Engaged? Wait, it wasn't too long ago that you were here for the wedding and you didn't tell me anything about you even being involved with anyone."

"I wanted the focus to be on you and your big day. By the time I thought about it, I needed to get back home to work," Victoria lied. She hoped she sounded convincing.

Victoria could hear clapping on the other end of the phone. She must have the phone on speaker.

"Congratulations!" Tajia said, obviously ecstatic for her friend.

"Who is this lucky fella? This guy must have really swept you off of your feet."

It's now or never, Victoria thought.

"The lucky fella is Turner, Taija," she said, waiting for the tons of questions from Taija that she was sure would follow.

"Turner? Wait, you two have been seeing each other? Since when? How did that happen? You've been friends since forever. When did the love happen? Why didn't you tell me?"

Tons of questions just as she expected.

"Taija, it just happened. After you left to move back to Atlanta, he and I began hanging out a lot more and we just sort of fell in love," she lied again.

Taija once lived in Boston which is where she and Victoria met. Taija had gone through a bad breakup in a relationship and needed some space. She'd taken a job in

Boston at the same company that employed Victoria and they had hit it off as friends from the first day. After Taija was offered a great job opportunity back in Atlanta where she had lived before Boston, she met and fell in love with her husband and they were soon going to be parents to a set of twins. It was because of Taija's recommendation that Victoria was able to move up in the company and really prove herself. Taija was highly regarded at the company and knowing that Victoria received her training from Taija, the powers that be put their trust in her, believing she could continue the work Taija had started, and she had.

"That's wonderful Victoria. I'm happy for you both. Are you bringing Turner to the baby shower?"

"Yes, that's why I'm calling. First I wanted to be sure it was okay that I bring him with me and second, I didn't want you to find out about the engagement when we got there."

"Girl, of course you can bring him. Have you set a date?"

"No, not yet. His family has known for a few weeks, but I just told my family today and now I'm telling you. You know the kind of money Turner comes from so this engagement will be big news. I didn't want those closest to me to read about it in the paper."

"Thanks for thinking of me. I hope you set your date well after the twins have been born and I can have time to get some of the weight off. I can't be the fattest one at your wedding," Taija laughed.

"Taija, girl, don't worry about it. You do mean in my wedding right and not just at it? I want you to be the matron of honor."

"Of course. Anything for you. I'm so happy for you.

Wait until I tell Duron. He'll be happy for you too," Taija added.

"Don't worry about any weight loss either. We haven't even set a date yet, but I'm sure it won't happen before the babies are born. For now, let's focus on you and my godchildren and we'll get back to me much later."

"That sounds like a plan. Speaking of godchildren, did I tell you that you would be sharing your role as a godparent with Tyrone, one of Duron's best friends and with Mike and Loren too? You may remember them all from my wedding."

Victoria definitely remembered them, especially Tyrone and hearing his name, a hot flash visual appeared in her mind of his bright, white smile as he lowered his head between her legs with that devilish look in his eyes. Victoria could never forget him. He had her climbing up the bed that night.

"Yes, I remember them. I'm looking forward to co-god parenting with him. Is that even a word?" Victoria asked as she and Taija laughed.

"They'll all be here at the shower also, so all of you can get together and talk about how you plan to spoil my children."

"That I can do," Victoria added. "I'll be coming in a day early to help your mother, Duron's mother and Loren get everything all set up for the shower. I can't wait to see you. Also, are you sure it's okay for me to stay at your house, especially now that I'm bringing Turner with me? He and I can always stay at a hotel."

"Nonsense Victoria. I want you here and we have a lot of catching up to do. There is plenty of room and I've already had things set up for you. Turner is more than welcomed to stay also."

"Okay, well I just wanted to let you know about the engagement. Also, Turner will be leaving on Sunday morning, but I'm staying until Wednesday so that we can have some girl time. I won't make it back that way until after the babies are born. I know you need your rest so I'm going to let you go. I'll see you soon."

"Okay and Duron will have a car picking you up so look for someone holding a sign up with your name when you land at the airport. Love you girl and I'll see you when you get here."

"Love you too," Victoria replied.

Now that she'd told her family and Taija, Victoria felt a little better. Now she needed to figure out a way to deal with Tyrone. She didn't know that he was also one of the godparents, though she should have expected it. He was, after all, one of Duron's best friends.

She was concerned about his reaction to finding out that the night they'd spent pleasuring each other like she'd never experienced before, she'd been engaged the entire time. Even though the engagement was fake, Tyrone won't know that. She couldn't tell him, which meant, in his eyes, she deliberately hid her engagement from him and slept with him anyway.

Since she lives in Boston and he lives in Atlanta, she would only have to deal with him for a few days after he found out and she could certainly handle that. She would just have to find a way to avoid him while she's in Atlanta. That's what her mind was saying, but her body was giving off a totally different vibe as she disconnected the phone and went in search of a very cold shower.

Chapter 6

Tyrone was working on one of his cars in his custom built garage after leaving the office early. It was the night before the baby shower, making it a few weeks since he'd seen and spoken to Victoria. He'd wanted to talk to her since his return from Texas, but decided to wait. He would be seeing her soon enough. He knew that she was scheduled to arrive in Atlanta earlier in the day. Duron mentioned sending a car to the airport to pick her up. He also mentioned that Victoria would be staying at his house while she was here. He couldn't wait to see her and to find out why she disappeared on him.

His cell phone rang just as he was about to slide underneath his recently acquired silver Porsche 550 Spyder, the same type of car that had been owned by the late actor James Dean. This car was an unexpected purchase after securing the Thunderbird. The same seller told him about the Porsche and he couldn't resist so he purchased both of them. He now owned five vintage cars, which now brought his car collection total up to seven including his own two, newer rides, his Mercedes and his Navigator truck.

"Hello," he said without looking to see who was calling.

"Hi son," his grandmother said.

Tyrone perked right up. He loved his grandmother more than anything. She'd raised him when his mother decided she didn't want him anymore.

"Gram, how are you?"

"I'm fine. I'm just checking on you. It was good to see you when you were in Texas recently. Every time you visit, I miss you more and more when you leave."

Tyrone's grandmother lived in Texas and during his recent business trip, he had gone out two days early to spend some time with her. He would do anything for her.

"I'm fine. I'm in the garage working on a car as usual," he said.

"I should have known without you even telling me. You and those cars. I hope you're being safe when you're out riding. You know I worry about you and how fast you drive."

"Gram it's only fast to you because you drive so slow," Tyrone said and laughed. "I promise you I am being very careful."

"That's good."

Tyrone became concerned when his grandmother had become quiet.

"Is everything okay?" he asked.

"Yes it is. I do have something I want to talk to you about."

The change in her tone made him get up so that he could give her his undivided attention.

"What is it Gram?"

"It's about your mother," he heard her say hesitantly.

At the mentioning of his mother, bile rose up in his throat. He hated thinking about and talking about the woman who walked away from him as an infant and never looked back.

"Gram, I love you, but you know that's a sour subject for me. I don't want to talk or even think about her," he said, clearly upset.

"I know son, I know. It's been a lot of years. Aren't you ever going to let that go?"

Tyrone knew she was right, but he couldn't seem to shake his discontent with his birth mother.

"I can't, at least not yet," he said, disappointed that no matter how much time had passed, he still couldn't forgive his mother for turning her back on him.

Tyrone was two years old when his mother disappeared from his life. One day she was there, the next she was gone. His grandmother was very honest with him about the circumstance. She didn't want him growing up with some made up story, only to one day find out the truth and have her regret not being honest with him.

She'd told him that his mother had gotten pregnant on purpose by a married man because she wanted him to leave his wife for her. His mother tried for two years to use him as a pawn in her game of getting the man away from his wife. When she realized it wasn't going to work, she left him with his grandparents, saying she didn't want to be a mother and they never heard from her again. Over the past year, his mother started showing up and his grandmother was trying to get them to work things out. His mother was very apologetic and riddled with guilt, but Tyrone couldn't find a forgiving bone in his body. He didn't know who his father was and he believed his grandmother when she told him she didn't know either. All she knew was that he was married and that he was mixed race, adding his seed to Tyrone's exotic look. His grandmother was Asian and his grandfather was African American making his mother of Asian and African American descent. There were tons of nationalities floating around in his blood. He loved his heritage and he loved hearing the stories of family from his grandmother. What he didn't like was hearing anything about the woman who only birthed him to win the love of a man who clearly didn't want her.

"Son, just think about it. I've spoken to her a few times recently and she really wants to see you. She wants to talk to you and hopefully mend a few fences with you," his grandmother said, almost pleading.

Tyrone loved his grandmother, but his heart was already as hard as stone when it came to his mother and he wasn't ready yet.

"Gram, I really can't right now, but I won't say never. I love you too much to say never, especially since I know how much it means to you."

He loved his grandmother and he would normally do anything for her except forgive his mother. His grandmother was the one constant in his life growing up. After his grandfather died, it was just the two of them until he'd gone off to college.

"That's all I ask," his grandmother said. "Just think about it and try to find it in your heart to forgive her. I know what she did was wrong and it hurt you, but you can't walk around with this hurt forever. It will taint your outlook on life and on women. I still say it's why you haven't had a lasting relationship yet. All women are not like your mother. Not every relationship has an ulterior motive," Tyrone heard his grandmother say.

Tyrone should have known that his grandmother would eventually turn the conversation to his personal life. She often commented on his proclivity for dating woman after woman without any kind of commitment, thinking that they would all eventually turn out to be heartless like his mother and he didn't want to open himself up for that type of hurt. He decided that he would never let anyone get that close to him.

"Gram, are you about to use this as an opportunity to politic for a granddaughter and great grandchildren? I told you that's not me and that hasn't changed," he informed her.

"I know, I know. I've heard the story. Anyway, I wanted to say hello. I'll let you get back to your cars. I love you son," he heard her say just before hanging up the phone.

Tyrone loved cars and motorcycles. Of course he loved new styles, but his passion was in collecting older, vintage type cars and his collection was growing. He was thankful that he was skilled at making upgrades to cars. It was a way for him to deal with frustrations that came his way, especially when thoughts of his mother crept up over the years.

He dealt with frustrations that he'd never even told his best friends about and he couldn't think of a better way to bang them out than on a car or two.

As he once again slid back under his Porsche, he realized he had a lot of frustrations to bang out. His mother was trying to get back into his life and he didn't want to deal with that. Another frustration was that he would be seeing Victoria the next day. Seeing her he could deal with, but his reaction to seeing her again, he wasn't as sure about. He hadn't been able to stop thinking about her since their one night together and that was unlike him. He usually had no problem moving on from a night of good sex with a woman, but there was something about Victoria he couldn't shake. It was that something that caused his frustration as he began banging away at repairs to the Porsche.

~~

Victoria and Loren were putting finishing touches on the decorations for the baby shower. She was glad the shower was at Duron's house so that Taija wouldn't have to go out. She was excited to see Taija and was happy at how she glowed from the pregnancy. She was carrying the babies well, but Victoria could see she was getting tired from the extra weight of carrying two babies.

"I like Turner a lot," Loren said to Victoria.

"Yeah, he's a good guy. We've known each other since childhood," she said.

"Sounds like a fairy-tale story," Loren added before turning to help her mother carry more bags into the room to unpack even more decorations.

Victoria loved how the decorating was turning out. The back patio part of the house was transformed into a zoo. Not with real animals, but with tons of decorations of animals from blowups of them to gigantic stuffed ones. Animals was the theme being used in the bedroom she had seen the night before that Taija showed her. That room would be the babies' room.

Victoria looked around and spotted Turner helping the men set up extra tables while the women continued setting up the decorations and helping with the food. With the help of Jason, one of Duron's friends who owned a popular Atlanta supper club, the food was laid out as if they were preparing for a huge feast.

Victoria was so distracted looking around at everything that when she turned to go back into the house to get the tableware, she walked right into a massive wall of nothing but glorious chest. She recognized that wall immediately. *Tyrone.*

She would have stumbled backwards if he hadn't reached out to brace her before she could do so.

"Hello, Victoria," she heard him say in his deep baritone voice. She remembered that voice and obviously her body did as well. It reacted to it with a slight quiver.

"Hello, Tyrone," she replied.

"You look beautiful."

"Thank you," she responded nervously.

"So you weren't a dream," he said. "I figured I must have dreamt you up when I woke up in the morning and discovered no trace of you."

Tyrone spoke softly so that no one else could hear him but her.

He leaned in even closer to her ear, looking around first to be sure no one was paying attention to them.

"If it hadn't been for the many, many condom wrappers I'd thrown away that morning, I would have thought that you were a figment of my imagination, but here you are and in my arms again."

Before Victoria could say anything, Loren appeared, breaking into the moment just as she'd stepped out of Tyrone's embrace.

"Ty," Loren said walking over to give him a hug. "I'm glad you could make it. I see you found Victoria. I hear you two ran into each other in Texas recently," she said looking from Victoria to Tyrone, not missing what appeared to be a very awkward moment.

Tyrone noticed the awkwardness and tried his best to alleviate it. He stepped back further away from Victoria and drew Loren into what was now a circle of the three of them.

"Yes, we sure did."

He looked Victoria in the eyes.

"We ran into each other a few times."

He spoke, hoping Victoria would catch on to the double meaning behind his words.

Clearing her throat and her mind, Victoria found her voice to speak.

"Yes, we did and it was good seeing him. I thought I recognized him, but I wasn't quite sure since I'd only met him at the wedding and here he is again," she said, not able to take her eyes off of his gorgeous face.

It was clear that Loren was oblivious to what she walked in on as she told Tyrone she needed his help with something and moved about busily in the kitchen grabbing things.

"Sure," he said to her request.

"I'll be back Victoria," he said before walking off.

Victoria stood, staring at his retreat wondering how she would survive the baby shower if he continued to make references to their night together. The reaction she'd had to him in Texas had not waned any. His presence brought on feelings of want and desire as they had that night in Texas and even now, her body tingled every place he touched.

She was in trouble.

Her view of Tyrone became obstructed by the presence of Turner.

"Hey you," he said.

Victoria jumped at his sudden appearance.

"Hey yourself," she said.

"Your friends are very nice and Taija looks lovely. I hadn't seen her since she left Boston. She has changed a lot. She used to be sullen and now she's all bright, cheery and happy. I guess love does that to you."

"Maybe one day we'll both find love like that," Turner said.

Victoria knew what he meant. He was making reference to their fake engagement and how they'd both struggled with many relationships that never led anywhere.

Victoria felt a little choked up. She definitely wanted that. She would give up a year to help her friend and she hoped after that, she would have the kind of love every little girl dreams of.

"Yeah, one day," she replied before telling Turner she needed to go grab things to continue with the setup.

Chapter 7

Throughout the shower, Tyrone kept his eyes on Victoria. He tried to be sly about it, in hopes that no one else noticed his fascination with her. The place was packed with people, but his focus was drawn to one person. She was one of the hosts for the party so she'd had a lot to do. She ran around all day helping Taija and Duron's mothers with all of the shower necessities. Loren was helping too, but being pregnant herself, Mike forced her to sit still and take things easy after a while. She was still recovering from a major injury due to being hit by a car, he reminded her.

Tyrone took a few minutes to admire all that was going on around the tent when he heard someone call his name.

"What?" he asked, clearly having no idea what was going on.

"I said come up here for a minute," he heard Taija say. She was sitting in the center of the tent, opening some of her many, many gifts. He put his beer down on a nearby table before heading in her direction. He also noticed Victoria also making her way to the front of the tent along with Mike and Loren. Duron was already sitting in a chair next to Taija helping her open gifts.

When everyone reached the front, Taija introduced the four of them to everyone as the godparents to the twins. Excitement broke out as everyone celebrated what will clearly be two very spoiled children. Not spoiled in a bad way, but spoiled with more than enough love. When they were about to return to their seats, Taija spoke again.

"I also wanted everyone to say one more round of congratulations. Victoria here, one of my dearest friends from Boston is engaged to be married."

Applauds went up all around the place. Tyrone wasn't sure he heard her at first until Taija asked Victoria's fiancé to stand. Tyrone recognized him as the guy he'd been introduced to earlier when he arrived. No one mentioned then that he was here with Victoria or that they were engaged. He thought the guy may have been a co-worker of Taija's or a family friend. He continued to listen to Taija who was clearly full of revelations today.

"It appears my friend has been engaged for a few months now and just got around to telling me recently. I won't hate on her too much for keeping her engagement from me for so long since she asked me to be the matron of honor at her wedding. After the twins are born and I've dispensed of some of this baby weight, I look forward to supporting her just as she has always supported me," Tyrone heard her say with excitement.

Everyone shouted rounds of congratulations except Tyrone. He was shocked and he had no doubt it showed on his face when he looked right at Victoria who happened to be looking directly at him with a look that said she was sorry he had to find out this way. He knew she was thinking the same thing that he was; she was engaged the night they'd spent wrapped around each other. Yes, she was engaged, Tyrone thought, and she never said anything about it.

His total shock made his feet feel like they were glued to the ground. He was stuck in his current spot and couldn't take his eyes off of Victoria, standing in the front of the tent, looking at him very uncomfortably.

"Let's see the ring," someone shouted.

Tyrone looked as everyone else did at the huge rock that sat on Victoria's left hand. It was a ring he would have noticed if she'd been wearing it in Texas. It's obvious she deliberately deceived him by hiding it. His last thought before exiting the tent and heading back into the house was, what kind of game was Victoria trying to play?

He was standing off to the side when Victoria and Loren entered the kitchen.

"Hey, Ty. We were all wondering where you disappeared to. Victoria and I came in to get more deviled eggs from the fridge and to heat up a few more rolls," Loren said.

He deliberately didn't open his mouth to respond, not trusting what would come out. While Loren continued talking, he again had his eyes on Victoria who tried to act as if she didn't notice his stare.

"I'll take the eggs out Victoria. Why don't you go ahead and heat up the rolls. I'll send someone from Jason's staff back in to help you bring them out."

Loren grabbed the trays from the fridge and went back out the way she came.

Tyrone noticed Victoria's nervousness at the thought of being left alone with him. He moved more into the room.

Victoria wasn't sure she was breathing. She didn't know

what to say to him. She knew his thoughts had to be on her engagement and she didn't have an answer for him if he asked her why she never mentioned it. She decided to do what she came into the kitchen to do and as long as he didn't say anything, she wouldn't either. That silence didn't last long.

"Congratulations," Tyrone said, not really meaning it, but trying to ease his way into a conversation about her pending marriage.

Victoria didn't know how to respond, so she didn't.

Her silence angered him.

"I don't even get a thank you?" he asked, moving even closer to her as she placed rolls in a pan on the counter. He came up behind her, not quite touching her, but allowing the heat from his body to flow her way.

"What are you doing Tyrone?" she asked uneasily.

The heat clearly wasn't coming from the stove which she knew was turned on, though she felt like she was in the middle of a sauna.

"I'm not doing anything but congratulating you on an engagement that has been going on for months I think Taija said?"

He then moved back from her and went around to the other side of the island, leaning against the counter so that he could look directly at Victoria as they spoke.

Victoria knew she shouldn't, but she looked up and over at him anyway. What she saw looking back at her was intense anger and confusion. She didn't know how to start explaining the situation, knowing she couldn't tell him the truth.

She couldn't seem to take her eyes off of him looking sexy, leaning against the counter, legs crossed, in a pair of denims that were clearly defining the package she remembered very well from their night together. The heat was definitely rising and there was no controlling it. His stance alone was driving her crazy. All she could think about were those bowed, hairy legs that ran up to his taut behind, the very same one she remembered grabbing and holding on to as he entered her body over and over again, making her scream until she was hoarse.

"What are you doing Tyrone?" she asked again.

"I already answered that. I'm standing here doing nothing at all except congratulating you on your engagement," he said in a sexy southern, Texas drawl.

"You're doing more than that."

"Am I making you uncomfortable by standing here Victoria?"

The way he said her name made her shudder. She thought back to their night together and the number of times he'd said her name seductively in her ear letting her know how she felt to him as he moved in and out of her. It was the way he would say her name that took her over the edge again and again. She shook her memories off. She had to stop going back to that night. It wasn't good for either of them if she couldn't let go.

"Thank you," Victoria said, finally acknowledging his congratulations. She thought, maybe if she said it, he would go away and leave her with her guilt.

Before he could say anything else, she tried to end the tension in the room.

"We can't do this here, Tyrone."

"Do what here, Victoria. I am merely standing here. If my memory serves me correctly, I was already standing here when you came into the kitchen, so if there is a level of discomfort, you are bringing it on yourself."

"I didn't know you were in here."

"True, but since you've now been in here for a few, you obviously didn't make the choice to run for the hills, so again, any level of discomfort can be minimized by you going back out the way you came. I'm not stopping you," he said with a little more anger than he wanted to.

Tyrone watched as she pretended to be occupied with putting the rolls in the pan.

Silence ensued as they stood, both sensing the elephant in the room.

"So, you're engaged to be married and sporting an enormous ring I don't think I remember seeing before. Isn't that something," he said.

The lack of response from Victoria did not escape him so he continued on figuring sooner or later he would say something that would get more of a rise out of her. Though he was standing being as calm and cool as he could be, he was actually pissed off at her deceit. He didn't like being used. He pushed things up a notch and went in for the kill.

"Imagine my shock at hearing that the woman who rode me like a stallion from sun down until sun up was engaged when she had done so."

He saw her body tense up. Jackpot he thought.

"Stop it," he heard her say on a whisper. "Anyone could hear you."

"Are you afraid lover boy out there would hear me mention how you allowed me to lick every single, solitary inch of your incredible body and not once before, during or after did you mention you were engaged or that you belonged to another man?"

Victoria heard the words coming out of his mouth, but what she saw were images of what he was saying and how good it felt to have his tongue pleasuring her for hours.

Tyrone watched as embarrassment crossed Victoria's face.

"Oh that's right, I meant before or during because we both know what happened after. You disappeared to run back to your fiancé in Boston."

She did not miss the extra emphasis he'd placed on the word, fiancé.

"Don't Tyrone," she pleaded before turning around to place the rolls in the oven and to also avoid his piercing stare. She couldn't stand to see the disappointment that appeared on his face.

When she turned back around, she watched as he slowly walked back around toward her. Her feet felt like lead. She knew that she should move away, but his mere presence seemed to hypnotize her to the spot and she couldn't move.

"Don't worry your pretty little head about it sweetheart. The guys are all on the lower level and all of the ladies are still busy making a big fuss over all of the baby shower gifts for Taija," he said, finally coming to stand directly in front of her. Memories made her want to reach out and touch him and to pass her hands across the chest that was beckoning her to touch. She dare not even think of doing it so she balled her hands into fists at her side hoping that would halt any desire to reach out and touch him.

She held her breath as he leaned in closer, just a mere whisper away from her ear.

"I would never put you in an uncompromising position amongst all of these people here today, especially with

Turner, the fiancé, in tow. I do want you to know however, that fiancé or not, I have done nothing but think about you every single day since you left Texas. No matter what I do, I can't seem to get you off of my mind. Even right now while I'm pissed that you purposely disregarded telling me you were engaged, I wouldn't want to embarrass you or cause any kind of trouble."

Tyrone looked down at Victoria's hands balled up at her side.

"I'm assuming by the way your hands are balled up at your side that you feel the same way too or it wouldn't be such a struggle for you to resist me. I think we have unfinished business and I'm not talking about sex, unless you want that," he said slyly.

Victoria winced not in pain, but in pleasure as her body heated up with thoughts of what she wanted. She held her lips together afraid of what she may admit to while she listened to him continue.

"As you already know, I do aim to please. I know saying this to you now, knowing the circumstance, is wrong, especially with that big rock on your finger, but I can't resist. Angry or not, I still want you. I'm not saying it to put any pressure on you, but I would like to know why you didn't tell me you were engaged and why unlike today, you didn't have your ring on when I saw you in Texas."

He could sense she was about to offer up an explanation, but he cut her off before she had a chance to speak.

"I don't want anyone to walk in and wonder why we're standing so close to each other, so when you're ready to talk to me, let me know. When are you and Turner leaving town?" he asked, hoping he wasn't pushing the limits.

Victoria couldn't handle his stare anymore, especially with him standing so close to her. She also knew that Tyrone could see that her nipples were hard through the thin material of her shirt. She was embarrassed that she was displaying clear desire for him and her body's reaction to him was just as it had been in Texas. She turned around so that her back was to him to avoid looking at him. She needed to collect herself. When she did so, she tried to think before revealing too much information about her and Turner's stay in Atlanta, but her mouth moved before her mind thought it through.

"Turner is leaving tomorrow and I'm staying here with Taija until Wednesday," she said, timidly.

Tyrone was just as turned on by this shy Victoria he was experiencing as he was by the wild, free and aggressive Victoria he encountered in the hotel room.

He didn't say anything. When she turned her back to him, he moved closer to her, keeping his eye on the doorway to be sure no one saw them standing like this. He knew he shouldn't, but the connection between the two of them was electric. He was standing so close to her that the smell of her took him back to the night they were together. He remembered her scent and she was wearing the same perfume now.

He moved close enough that his front was pressed so close to her back that if they were naked, he would already be inside of her. He couldn't help himself even if he tried when he quickly snaked his tongue out of his mouth after making sure it was very moist, and licked around her earlobe before darting his tongue inside of her ear. He felt her body quake slightly knowing the effect that little act would have on her. He had already memorized the parts of her body that aroused her the most. He knew any connection with her ear was an erogenous zone.

"I see you remember my touch. As wrong as this may be, while you're here for the next few days I want to see you. You don't have to say anything, but I already know you. I can feel the heat radiating from your body through your clothes. You want to see me too don't you? Feel free to nod if you can't get the words out," he said seductively with much restraint. He was holding back from taking her upstairs and planting himself so deep in her, it wouldn't be noticeable that they were two separate people. He wanted her that much, engagement ring or not.

Victoria couldn't remember being this turned on in her life. She'd spent one magnificent night with this man, yet her body reacted as if it had been in tuned to his touch and his sound for a lifetime. She couldn't deny she wanted to see him alone again, but she couldn't. She did however owe him an explanation and this was not the time to discuss it so she simply nodded her agreement. She sensed his smile when he knew he had won. No further words were spoken.

Victoria actually felt shamefully disappointed when Tyrone turned away from her and exited the kitchen, heading to the lower level to meet up with the other guys who had ventured down there. Only then did she finally exhale.

Chapter 8

At the end of the night as everyone was leaving, Victoria noticed Turner talking to Tyrone, Mike and Duron. She had to know what they were talking about so she walked over to join them.

"Hey fellas," she said.

Turner reached out and pulled her up against his side.

"Victoria, I've been standing here talking to your friends and I can't believe you never told me about the business they owned. I was just telling them that I'd like to discuss a joint business venture with them, especially after I take over the family winery business," Turner said, more excited than Victoria ever remembered him being.

"I guess it just never came up," she said.

"Well it did tonight and I think we're going to be doing some business together."

That comment shocked her.

"Really," she struggled to say. "What kind of business."

"I was telling them all about the winery and the

vineyards in Washington and my plans for expanding not only the plants, but modernizing the office buildings as well. Tyrone here has agreed to fly up to Boston soon to meet with me to start the discussions and I can show him some of the ideas I have. I told them how we have plans to move back to Washington after our wedding and with your finesse in financing, you'd be joining the company not only as my wife, but as my partner in business as well. I'd like to get all the preliminary work done ahead of time so that once I take over everything, we won't have a lot of wasted time. Isn't that great?" he asked.

"Yeah, isn't that great, Victoria?" she heard Tyrone add in. She looked at him, pleading with her eyes for him to not reveal anything.

"We all think it's a great business opportunity all around," she heard Duron say.

She knew it could be great, but not on a personal level.

"I'm glad Tyrone volunteered to spearhead this one. I feel like we're putting a lot on him right now, but he said he wanted to do this one," Victoria heard Duron say while she tried to avoid the penetrating look Tyrone was giving her.

"Yes it is," she agreed. "I'm going to let you boys finish talking business while I help with the rest of the clean-up since most of the people are finally heading out," Victoria said right before turning on shaky legs away from the conversation. All she could think about was the fact that she didn't need Tyrone on her territory in Boston. She was already concerned about the impact of them all working together on a project while still holding on to the secret, not only of the circumstances behind her engagement, but holding on to the secret about the time she and Tyrone spent together in Texas. She feared the more time they spent around each other, the more someone may be able to sense something was going on between them. If that happened, she knew there would be hurt all around. As she walked away, she knew she was going to have to figure out a way to stay clear of Tyrone at all cost. That was the only way she knew she'd be able to fight the desire to repeat their night together.

~~

"Victoria, could you be a dear and check the lower level to be sure no plates, cans or other items are left? I know a few of the guys had been in the theater room earlier," Duron's mother asked her.

"Yes, sure," she agreed and went to check.

Victoria checked around the entire room and didn't see anything. She was heading back to the stairs to go back up when her heart skipped a beat at seeing Tyrone standing at the foot of the stairs leaning against the post looking sexier than any man should ever look.

She stopped in her tracks and neither of them said a word. In a move like something out of a movie, Tyrone seemed to glide across the room to her. No matter how he actually did it, he was standing in front of her, staring down at her with a look of pure lust.

This can't be happening she thought. They were once again alone. The looks between them spoke trouble and she wasn't sure she could fight what she was feeling. One of them had to have a level head.

"Don't Tyrone."

"Don't what Victoria," he said reaching up to caress the side of her face.

"I'm not so sure I can resist you," she stated pointedly.

"Why would you want to resist me," he drawled and her

will to resist him began falling away. She only experienced this reaction to him and she didn't understand it. This never happened to her before. It was as if her body didn't care what her mind was saying. It was reacting on its own.

"I have to because I'm engaged."

Tyrone laughed.

"So now you tell me you're engaged," he said reaching down and lifting her left hand to get a better look at her ring.

"That's a gorgeous ring. I like it a lot and it looks good on you," she heard him say as he lowered her hand once again to her side while raising his hand to lift her face up to look directly into his eyes.

"Do you know what else looks good on you?" he asked seductively and softly so that no one would be able to hear them if they happened to pass by the stairwell.

Victoria couldn't resist responding. She wasn't sure she could deny him anything, not even an answer.

"No. What else looks good on me," she whispered back softly.

"Me," he said, huskily. "I look good on you. I can tell by the slight shivering you're doing right now that I not only looked good on you, but I also felt good to you, on you, in you and under you as well. Am I wrong?" he asked, not being able to help himself.

There was something about being around Victoria that brought out the devil in him. No matter how wrong it felt standing here with her this way, knowing she belonged to another man, somewhere in the back of his mind one word kept playing over and over again. *Mine.*

Before she could respond to the image his response placed in her head, he leaned down and licked the crease between her lips, slowly from the left corner to the right, making her moan. He remembered what that moan meant. He never took his eyes off of hers while he repeated the seductive act again.

On his second pass, Victoria moaned again before she opened her lips, giving him the chance to slip his tongue inside. Once he did, a feeling of possession took over him. He pulled her body flush up against his and sunk in even deeper into her mouth. On his entry in, he started slow by dipping in, going further and further with each grip of his lips to hers while his tongue sought out hers, doing a happy duel. An inferno began to form in various parts of his body, all remembering her and what it felt like to be this close to her. The power behind the connection between the two of them felt like a hurricane. Their tongues were swirling with force and passion that was beginning to consume them both. Tyrone noticed that Victoria was just as much a participant as he was. She was gripping his forearms, holding on, trying to not lose her balance as she returned the kiss with just as much fervor as he was. The kiss was filled with hunger and they were equally moaning now trying to draw more and more from the kiss and from each other.

Tyrone pulled Victoria even tighter to his frame, allowing her to feel his hardness and how it was seeking her out. When she began grinding on his stiffness, Tyrone thought he saw stars. The feel was overwhelming.

They only stopped when the need to breathe took over.

When he could once again speak he turned her face up so that he could look deep into her eyes.

"Now, one thing I know is women. Another thing I know is when I look at Mike and Loren and Duron and

Taija there is no mistaking the love that is between them. There is no doubt how deep they care for and love each other. What I also know is the kind of passion we shared in Texas and what we just shared in that kiss was not something a woman can share with more than one man at a time. I don't know what's going on with you and Turner, but what I don't see is deep, uncontested, soul-stirring love. I also think that you are not the kind of woman who would let a man handle you the way I just did and you returned it with just as much fervor, if you were truly in love with another man and about to marry him."

Victoria gulped at the way Tyrone read her entire story. Of course he was right and she knew that there was something special she was sharing with him, something she had never before shared with any man before. It was unmistakable that the combination of him and her together was real. How could he read her so well, she thought to herself? She couldn't answer him. She couldn't find the words to speak.

"Victoria, I don't know what's going on here and you don't have to tell me. If I thought you were in love with Turner, I would not deliberately stake you out like this, but what I see between the two of you is not love; it's friendship. I've watched the two of you all evening. It's not lust, like I see looking back at me when I look at you, it's kindness. The kind that's developed out of years of close friendship, not intimacy. Intimacy and lust are what we shared. It's what I'm feeling right now. It's what I see as I look into your eyes. You are not a casual kind of woman going between two men. Now I like Turner, I like him a lot and I look forward to a great business partnership with him, but I like you even more. If I thought I was wrong here, I would back off. If you thought I was wrong here, you would tell me to back off, but right now, I can tell you want me just as much as I want you. Am I correct?" he asked, waiting to give her time to respond.

Victoria was overwhelmed by this man. She nodded her head in the affirmative.

"Are you going to tell me what's going on with you and Turner?" he asked, bringing her closer so that she was flush against his body once again, allowing her to feel the hard ridge of his erection through the light material of her skirt.

Again, she couldn't speak so she shook her head from left to right giving him a negative to that question. She also noticed his frustration with her response. He wasn't getting the answers he sought and she felt bad, but she had to keep the secret of the agreement she made with Turner. His future depended upon it and she couldn't let him down no matter how much she wanted to tell him the truth.

"Victoria, how can you want me so much and be engaged to another man? I don't understand that. I need to know what's going on here. Can't you see I'm on the edge here? I'm ready to push you back against this wall and give us both what I think we are craving. I don't want to hurt anyone, especially not you and not Turner, but the vibes are getting all mixed up between us," he crooned close to her lips.

She could feel it too as her head screamed no and yes at the same time. She wanted this man with a fierceness she had never encountered before. No matter how wrong she knew it was, she wanted him to back her up against the wall and give her what she had been dreaming about since she'd left Texas. It was all she had been able to think about and now that she was standing with him alone, the temptation was great. It was becoming uncontrollable and she didn't know how much more she would be able to resist. Before Tyrone could speak again and put more doubt between them, she reached up and grabbed the sides of his face and brought his mouth hungrily down on hers.

The kiss was electrifying. Tyrone showed no resistance as he gave her what she clearly needed from him. She was on fire and he was like fuel.

"Goodness, baby," he said, taking his lips away from hers.

He looked in her eyes and saw want on a level that he knew matched his.

"I don't know what's going on between us, but I can't help myself. I need you baby. I need you so bad right now. I know this is wrong and I'll probably burn in hell for this, but there is no way I can leave this room and not have you first."

Victoria, still unable to speak because she was afraid she would doubt her actions and not get what she wanted and needed as bad as he did showed no sign of resisting whatever he had in mind.

Before he could say another word, she reached for the hem of his shirt, tugging it out of his jeans, all the while, not taking her eyes off of his. After she had his shirt out, she ran her hands up under it, basking in the pleasure of once again feeling her hands all over his muscular chest. She had memories of licking and kissing all over that chest and it sent her body on a whole new level of yearning.

Tyrone didn't question what they were doing. Victoria apparently had no doubts about what she wanted to do and she wanted to take the lead to let him know that if he were second guessing what they were about to do, he shouldn't.

He went into action knowing they needed to move quickly. Soon everyone would see that they were missing and he didn't want any awkward moments.

He quickly moved them into a part of the room that was the furthest from the steps.

When Victoria felt the wall at her back, she exhaled and her heart raced with excitement. This was all she had been able to think about since returning after that night with Tyrone. Her mind had been consumed with thoughts of him since that night.

Everything else happened in a flash. Tyrone reached up under her skirt to test her readiness for him and was happy to see that there was no doubt she was ready. He could imagine her needing to ring her panties out because one swipe of his finger across her womanhood had her moisture running down his finger and pooling in his palm.

He was overwhelmed with the need to be inside of her that he needed to catch his breath by leaning his forehead down against hers looking for the strength to pull away. This wasn't him. He didn't go after women already taken.

"Dammit Victoria, tell me to stop. I don't think I can on my own because I want you too bad. The longer we stand like this and you allow me to touch you like this, the harder it is for me to turn around and head back up the steps, which I know is exactly what I should do."

"I can't stop you because I don't want to."

"I can feel the proof of how much you want me and I'm standing here harder than I've ever been for any woman in my life. I seem to get like this with just the thought of you, so tell me this is wrong. Tell me to release you and go back upstairs so that you can return to your fiancé," he pleaded.

He winced at the thought that she had a fiancé, but he knew he needed her to say it because if she uttered anything that resembled she didn't want him to release her, he was done for.

Victoria couldn't hold back anymore. She would deal with the consequences later.

"Tyrone, I'm sorry for not telling you I was engaged. I wanted you so much that night that nothing else entered my mind, not even the fact that I was engaged. My want for you took over, just as it's doing right now. I'm just as wrong as you are here, but like you, I can't help myself either. I need to feel you inside me. I need to feel what I felt back in Texas. I know how much you want me and I know it's wrong, but please don't deny what we both know we want."

She reached to unbuckle his pants while continuing to look at him.

"I want you now," he heard her say with force. He recognized that aggressiveness that he remembered. It was back and he loved it.

"Victoria if we do this, there is no turning back," he said, trying to give her a chance to have the level head.

He didn't have to wait long for the answer that didn't come in the form of words. Instead he leaned back, looked directly into Victoria's eyes and saw nothing but want and a passionate desire staring back at him. With that look came the feel of Victoria using her fingers to trace the hard ridge of his erection through his pants. He leaned his head back, closing his eyes trying to fight through the feelings. His mind was reeling with thoughts of how wrong this situation was, but he was losing the fight. His body, over his mind was in charge and he knew he was a lost cause.

He knew that if she'd told him to walk away, he would because he didn't want to hurt her or put her in a position that was uncomfortable.

The decision was made the moment she unzipped his jeans all the way.

"Victoria are you sure? I have spent a countless number of hours thinking about you touching me like this and most of those thoughts have occurred since we arrived here at the shower tonight. I won't apologize or say I'm sorry even when I know your situation. I would never compromise another man's woman because I definitely wouldn't want it done to me if I were in his shoes, but I can't help myself; I want you."

"Tyrone, there is something about you that I just can't seem to resist. I could say it was just the incredible sex I know we would have, but it's not just that. At this moment I can't think of anything except you being inside of me. I know this is a terrible time and a terrible place for this, but I want you right here, right now. Please don't make me wait anymore. We can talk another time about things, but not right now. I may end up talking myself out of this and I don't want to do that. I want you," she pleaded, hoping that was enough to reassure him that she was all in.

She didn't wait for anymore words as she reached inside of his pants for that part of him that was seeking her out like a heated military missile.

Victoria couldn't believe she was standing in the home of one of her best friends, with her fiancé one floor away about to open up her body to the pleasure she couldn't stop thinking about since she'd last experienced it.

Her temperature rose several degrees as she retrieved that part of him that she remembered so well. His member felt hard and heavy under her touch and when she pulled him all the way out and ran her hand up and down both sides of his ridged flesh, she felt him jump in her palm. As much as she wanted to take her time and pleasure him again in more ways than she could count, they didn't have time for all of that. Soon someone may come looking for them and she couldn't leave without getting the release that her body so desperately wanted and needed.

"Hurry Tyrone. I can't take the torture much longer," she said with an urgency she had never heard come from her lips before.

"I aim to please, baby," he said, drawing a condom from his back pocket and putting it on. Before either of them could catch their next breath, he reached down to grasp both of her legs in both of his hands and pressed her back into the wall. He drew her up the wall so that her slick entrance was poised right over his straining hardness.

In a swift move, he slid her panties to the side and in one strong surge, he entered her.

Victoria sighed on the entry, not believing she was once again experiencing what she had been desiring for weeks. It was that feeling of him sliding all the way inside almost touching her womb. She didn't have to remember how long and thick he was. His entry into her body stole her breath, reminding her of his girth. He felt so good she wanted to cry out with pleasure. She assumed he could tell she was about to do just that because he took that cry of pleasure into his own mouth when he took her mouth in a deep, penetrating kiss to contain the scream that was ready to escape her lips.

While they engaged in a kiss that sent chills up her spine, she began riding up and down on him as he pumped up into her.

Tyrone's mouth, like the lower part of his body, was taking complete control of her senses and she reveled in the feel of him. She couldn't seem to get enough as the tension of the climax began to surface while she bucked up and down on him like a stallion in heat.

"That's it baby. Squeeze me with your muscles and get everything you need from me," he said on a groan, holding back his own release until after Victoria had climaxed.

"Yes, Tyrone, give it to me. Give me all of it," she whispered in his ear as she chased the orgasm that was just within her reach.

"Can you hear the sounds of how wet you are with every pass of me in and out? The sounds are music to my ears baby. Are you ready? I want you with me. Are you ready Victoria," Tyrone said as he pumped relentlessly into her over and over, her wetness running down the inside of his legs.

"Yes," she said, trying once again to not scream out her of pleasure.

"With me, right now, baby. Come on," was the last they both remembered before they climaxed together.

Victoria felt that quiver in her belly that she had only experienced with Tyrone. It was the sign that she was about to be hit with an explosion of pleasure like never before. When it finally hit, she bit down into Tyrone's shoulder to mask the scream that threatened to alert everyone in the house of what they were up to.

Victoria rode out her release just as she felt Tyrone reach his as well.

Tyrone rode out his release while moaning through it in the crook of Victoria's neck. He wanted to scream himself, but remembered, even while his climax continued on and on, that they were in the house of his best friend, with a room full of people above them.

When their breathing had returned to normal, Tyrone slid Victoria back down the wall, letting go of her legs so that they were relaxed. He had been holding them up the whole time for a deeper, more penetrating feeling.

Neither of them spoke as they attempted to fix their clothing and they never took their eyes off of each other while doing so.

Tyrone didn't know why, but the guilt he thought he would feel making love to a woman engaged to another man didn't happen. Did he just say making love? He didn't say sex? That was because he knew he had just made love to her and it wasn't just sex. He was already feeling things for Victoria that he had never felt for any other woman and it wasn't just sex; it was more than that.

"Are you okay, Victoria?" he asked. He watched as she looked down to be sure her clothes were once again back in place.

"I'm not talking about your clothes. I'm talking about you," he said with caring in his voice.

Tyrone was right. Something was happening between the two of them and it felt good, but it was also so wrong. Turner, who as far as Tyrone was concerned, was her fiancé was upstairs while she stood here already craving this man again. No she wasn't alright. She was a mess and she wasn't speaking about her clothes either, but she didn't want him to know that.

"Yes, I'm fine. Are you okay," she inquired.

"Yes, I am perfectly fine. We need to talk Victoria. I'm serious. I don't want to make anything uncomfortable for you, but can we still get together before you go back to Boston in a few days?"

Victoria looked at him, thinking he was talking about sex.

He lightened the mood when he smiled brightly at her, knowing what she must be thinking.

"I'm talking about to talk, not sex. I'm thinking just dinner or drinks or something, someplace very public."

"I agree, we should talk. Write your number down and I'll call you," she said.

He nodded his agreement while he pulled out one of his business cards and handed it to her.

"My cell is on here. You'd better go upstairs first. I would suggest heading for the restroom first. As hard as you came," he said in a voice laden with pure sex, "I'm sure you'll be uncomfortable with your essence running down your legs every time you walk."

Victoria smiled at the thought of what he'd just said. She couldn't doubt him one bit. That was a powerful orgasm.

She walked toward the steps and was pulled back before she reached the first one.

He needed one last kiss from her before he let her walk away from him and she obliged him. The kiss, though it should not have, held the promise of more to come. The kiss was telling her that this wasn't over for him and from the way she reacted to him, it wasn't over for her either.

Tyrone watched as she finally walked away. He turned and grabbed a seat in the theater room to try and take in all that had just happened. He loved women more than most men, but never in his life had he ever had to sneak and he didn't like it. He wanted Victoria, but sneaking around, he wouldn't do. There was something not right about the engagement between Victoria and Turner and he needed to find out what it was. If his hunch was correct, she wasn't in love with Turner and he was just as sure of himself that no wedding would be taking place. He needed to get to the bottom of things and he needed to do it soon. There was no way he had any plans of staying away from her, Turner or no Turner.

Chapter 9

Victoria spotted Tyrone sitting on a bench along the water waiting for her. Her heart raced at the thought of what they had done the night before at the baby shower. She was glad no one was able to tell what she had been up to when she rejoined everyone following the explosive orgasm she experienced with Tyrone in the theater room at Duron's house. She thought about it all night until she fell asleep. She got a few hours of sleep before getting up to take Turner back to the airport. He had business to attend to back in Boston. She left the airport and came straight to the park to meet Tyrone. She'd sent him a text before heading to the airport to see if he could meet that morning. It was his idea for them to talk and Victoria knew she wouldn't be able to avoid it. She wouldn't tell him everything, but she agreed they needed to talk.

"Hello Victoria. I'm glad you came," Tyrone said as he stood from the park bench as she walked up. "Would you like to sit down?"

"Sure," she said nervously, taking a seat.

"You look lovely," he said.

"Thank you."

After Tyrone had once again taken a seat on the bench, they sat staring at each other with no one speaking. Even though it was Tyrone's idea that they talk, Victoria decided to go first.

"Look Tyrone, I'm sorry. I know I should have told you about Turner when we were in Texas and I don't have an excuse or a story of why I didn't, so all I can do is say I'm sorry. You deserved to know before anything happened between us."

He heard the sincerity in her voice and knew she meant it. What he didn't know was why the ruse of not wearing the engagement ring and not hesitating when he suggested they go back to his room. They flirted shamelessly with each other throughout dinner and he was sure they were on the same page. There was no doubt they both wanted each other with a fierceness that only sweating it out between the sheets was going to cure.

"Is that why you disappeared without saying goodbye?" he asked.

"Partly and I also felt ashamed," she admitted.

Tyrone looked at her with a side eye, questioning look.

"Not ashamed of what we did, if that's what you are thinking, but ashamed because I knew there was a reason we should not have but you didn't," she said, not missing the confused look Tyrone was giving her.

"I enjoyed every minute of being with you. It didn't start with the hotel room. It started at the table over dinner. I was amazed at how much we had in common. I have never come across a man that I connected so well with and add in how sexy you are, I never doubted I wanted that one night stand as much as you did. I just didn't count on feeling like I'd done something wrong and deceitful by not telling you about Turner before we slept together. I know we agreed on a one night stand, but I shouldn't have left like I did without saying anything and for that I apologize."

Even now, her mind was thinking of how easy it would be to accompany him back to his place for a repeat of the night before, especially since Turner was on his way back to Boston. Stop it, she said to herself. Where were these wild thoughts coming from? This was unlike her. She'd never met any man who made her feel the things that she was feeling for Tyrone and that thought scared her more than it enticed her.

"Victoria, I appreciate you apologizing. I'm not sure one is needed because we did agree that it would be a one night stand, no strings and no explanations. I naughtily admit that my reason for being upset when I woke up and you weren't there was that I couldn't get a repeat of the night before since we were both returning to our lives. When I awoke and didn't see you, I tried to remember if maybe I had been dreaming and envisioned you."

He leaned over closer to her on the bench.

"Then I leaned over and I could smell you on the pillow and on the sheets and even on my skin. I knew you were there in that bed with me and I haven't stopped thinking about you since then. I even thought about asking for your number from Taija, but I didn't want to have to answer a lot of questions. I am glad to see you again, even though I now know you're engaged to marry Turner. I assume, even after last night, you still plan to marry him?" he asked not sure he really wanted to get an answer.

Victoria knew without a doubt that she planned to continue with her plans, but it was hard to explain things to Tyrone without telling him everything and she knew she couldn't do that.

"Yes I do. Listen, I really like you and I can't explain it considering my situation. Yes I'm engaged and yes I really like you, but what we shared back in Texas and last night can't change the plans that are already in place."

"Do you love Turner," he asked, not really wanting to hear that answer either.

"All of this is hard to explain," she said.

"I ask because you just said until you'd met me, you'd never connected with a man the way you have with me and that says something. It at least should make you question what's going on with you and Turner and what seems to continue to happen between you and I."

She blushed at the thought of what she and Tyrone shared the night before. He entered her life like a tornado and was causing a good kind of destruction in her life. Good because she loved how he made her feel and she'd longed for that type of relationship for a long time. She always thought that it would be unobtainable with the pool of men she dated over the years.

Tyrone saw the struggle in her and how uncomfortable the conversation was for her. He was putting her on the spot and that was not his intent. He decided to change the subject.

"Victoria, I'll tell you what, don't answer that. I didn't ask to speak with you to make you feel uncomfortable. For starters I did want an explanation and you sort of gave me that. I won't dig any further. I also wanted to see you again. I don't want you to think that when we see each other, I'm going to try and jump you. I admit that you are irresistible, but I will try my best to control myself," he said, smiling, hoping it would ease some of the tension.

She smiled and he felt better.

"I can't say that I won't want you, but I know that this can be very tricky, especially with the friendships we share. I don't want to cause you any drama and no grief. Let's take the tension out of everything so that over time, when we see each other, it won't be awkward. We will be around each other for years to come. We have godchildren coming soon and I have no doubt you'll want to be around them as much as I will. We have to find a way to make this work," he said.

The weight of his words set in. They were going to be around each other for years to come because of the connection through friendships they shared and because of the love they will both have for the godchildren they will share. They had to find a way to get beyond their current circumstance and move on.

"Thank you for that Tyrone. I appreciate that you see the bigger picture and I see it as well."

"Good," he said. "Now, how long are you in town for? I know you said Turner left today to return to Boston."

"I'll be here a few more days. I wanted to have a few days to hang with Taija and catch up. Work has been so busy lately that I don't get to talk to her as much as I want to."

"I'm sure she's glad you're here," Tyrone said, glad at the relaxed feeling of the conversation.

They sat chatting about all sorts of things for the next hour. He even told her about his latest car acquisition. Her face lit up and he promised to email her pictures of the car.

Victoria checked the time.

"I need to get back. Taija and I are having a girl's night in and I want to pick up a few things before heading back to the house. I'm glad we were able to talk Tyrone."

"So am I Victoria. It was good seeing you again. I need to get to my office. I still have a lot of work to catch up on, even on a Sunday."

He watched as Victoria stood, preparing to leave. He knew he made a promise that he would back off, but his mouth forgot that he'd said that and it seemed to open and speak on its own accord.

"Will you talk to me if I call you later tonight or you could give me a call anytime you're free to do so?"

Victoria knew that she would. As much as she knew she shouldn't, she, just like him, could not seem to resist him.

"Yes and I look forward to it Tyrone," she said. "I'll give you a call later this evening before I go to bed. Is that good for you?" she asked.

He knew he would take her any way he could get her.

"I look forward to it. Have fun during your girl's night," he said while walking Victoria back to Taija's car.

On the drive, Victoria knew without a doubt she was in trouble. She was finding herself much more attracted to Tyrone than she thought she would be. What was supposed to be a simple one night of unashamed, toe curling, hot as fire sex is now involving feelings and as much as she was enjoying it, time was not on her side. She promised her friend that she would help him out of a bind by marrying him, but how could she, when for once in her life, she finally found a man who was a total, complete package of everything she'd ever wanted in a man. Even though they only engaged in a few conversations, she enjoyed all of them. She was already aware of his great character. She learned a lot about Tyrone from Taija during the times that they would talk about Duron and his friends. What is a girl to do, she thought to herself. She was in a bind and normally this would be the perfect conversation to have with Taija, but she couldn't. She couldn't tell anyone that her engagement was fake, that she'd spent and unforgettable night with a man that she could see herself falling for and that for the first time since she agreed to this farce of a marriage with Turner, she was second guessing her decision. Her biggest problem was that she had no one to vent to.

~~

Tyrone had been anxious all evening hoping Victoria would call. His behavior was shocking to him. He never sweated over a woman and never over one engaged to another man, but there was something about Victoria that he just couldn't shake. He knew that she agreed to talk to him tonight and he looked forward to her call. Hearing her voice would top off his incredibly busy day.

He'd dated lots of women, but he never got close to any where he wanted to talk to them for more than to set up a date for sex. He wasn't ashamed of that. He'd had plenty of conversations with women up front, letting them know that he wasn't looking for a girlfriend or a relationship. He gave them pleasure that most never experienced before and he derived great pleasure in having his needs satisfied often.

With Victoria, things were different and he couldn't figure out why. There was something very odd about the relationship between Turner and Victoria and he felt even more so now than ever after their brief chat earlier in the day. If she were in love and ready to marry Turner, she wouldn't be confused and torn about what she was beginning to feel for him. He knew women and he could read her. She was into him even though she and Turner were engaged. He couldn't place his finger on it, but it was strange. He felt that he wasn't really coming between anything because he didn't see anything there. He'd watched them at the shower. They appeared to be more like best friends than lovers or an engaged couple. They never touched and they never displayed lingering looks like couples in love and about to be married often shared. Tyrone even remembered seeing Turner check out a few of Taija's sorority sisters who were in attendance at the shower. It wasn't just a passing glance either. It was the look a man gave a woman that he found attractive and was interested in. He recognized it because it was the same kind of look he had every time he saw Victoria.

His thoughts were still on the engaged couple as he showered and prepared to relax for the evening. The day was a long one and a nice cold beer was in his immediate future. His thought while at the office was to kick back at the condo he had on the top floor of the office park that housed their business. He, Duron and Mike each had a condo there, but he was the only one who didn't use his as much as the two of them did. He took great pleasure in being at his house where he could spend hours working on his cars, so instead of going up to his condo after finishing his work, he drove out to his house.

His mind was consumed with thoughts of Victoria all day as he found himself reading things over and over again, wasting much of his day and tiring him out from repeating tasks over, not accomplishing much.

As he walked around his house, this was the first time he realized just how empty it was. That never occurred to him before. With his grandmother living in another state and having no relationship with his mother or his father, unless he did things with Duron's family, there was no family around to invite over to enjoy this grand house he'd built.

It was too big for just him. He never thought of himself as the get married and have children kind of person. Any thoughts of that kind of life were ruined by the cruel treatment he received from his mother and the lasting effect it had on his life. He grew up longing for the love of his mother and he never received it. His grandmother tried to substitute her love with what he was missing, but it wasn't the same. His mother schemed and planned to snag his father and when that didn't work out, she high-tailed it out of town, leaving him with his grandparents. She never came around for birthdays or holidays and she went off to live her life without him, never looking back. He would never set himself up to care about a woman not knowing if she would decide one day that being with him was not what she wanted. That may be the reason he never wanted to get too involved with a woman. He wanted to be the one to control when things would be over.

His grandmother tried her best to get him to see that his mother was only one person and not all women would turn their backs on him, but he felt like he'd endured a lifetime of hurt from his mother and he would never open himself up to be hurt by another person, especially a woman.

Even while he felt that way, he thought of Victoria. He knew that she would love his house. She, like him, would fall in love with the garage area where he kept all of his cars, his motorcycles and the all-terrain vehicles he owned. He remembered how tuned in to her he was when she talked about an old car she loved as a little girl growing up. She told him she was planning to one day own the little white antique sports car. She talked about how she developed her love for cars from her own father who loved to play around with working on them in his spare time.

Tyrone could relate due to his love for cars.

He was still thinking about that as he relaxed in his man cave with his beer about to catch a movie when his cell rang. It was well after midnight and he knew it either had to one of his female friends, looking for a late night visit or it was Victoria. The latter was his preference as he reached to answer it.

"Hi Tyrone," Victoria's soft voice said.

"Hi Victoria. I'm glad you called."

"I'm sorry it's so late. Taija and I were talking well into the evening until Duron forced her to go to bed. She was nodding off for over an hour, saying she wasn't sleepy."

"Sounds like you ladies enjoyed a good time catching up," he said, laying back in one of the recliners in front of his big-screen television. He never did turn on the lights so the only light in the room came from the television that was now watching him.

"We did and I'm glad I made the trip from Boston. I've missed time spent with her catching up. We talk often over the phone, but it's not the same as in person."

"I'm glad you are getting this time with her. Life will soon change when those babies get here and I'm sure she'll spend all of her free time sleeping. Don't worry about how late it is. Feel free to call me anytime, day or night. I'll always take your call," he said.

The thought of being able to call him at any time excited her. She'd been thinking about him all evening. She loved being able to catch up with Taija because she hadn't seen her since the wedding and a lot had been going on that she wanted to share with her. She tried to focus all evening on the things they were talking about, including her wedding plans to marry Turner. She hated lying to Taija, but she wasn't ready to confess any truth about the situation to her either.

"So that means I didn't catch you at a bad time then?" she asked.

"No, not at all. I was just sitting here drinking a beer and relaxing."

"Well, how was your day? Did you get all the work done you needed to catch up on?"

She was trying her hand at idle chit chat even though her body began heating up the moment she heard his voice.

"Truth?" he asked.

"Yes, Tyrone, truth."

"No," he admitted. "I didn't get done as much as I wanted to. I couldn't stop thinking about you and I kept getting distracted."

"I'm sorry," she said.

"Why are you apologizing for my lack of concentration?" he said, smiling. What was it about this woman?

"I'm apologizing for being the reason you weren't able to have a productive day of work. I don't want to be the cause of any distractions for you. Do you think maybe we shouldn't talk at all?" she asked.

He definitely didn't want that.

"You being a distraction is not a bad thing even when it

applies to my lack of focus with work. I promised you I would try and back off and I'm going to do that. I just haven't started yet, so for today, my day was spent consumed with thoughts of you."

Victoria could relate. Even now, as she lay in bed at Taija's house, crossing and uncrossing her legs trying to relieve some of the pressure she was feeling between her legs, she knew the meaning of distraction. It started when she climbed into bed and grabbed her cell phone to call him. The excitement alone was enough to get her aroused. Even now, her desire for him had her thinking about reaching down with her hand to ease some of the ache.

"Victoria, are you there?" he said.

She didn't realize she wasn't talking because her concentration was on the ache and not on the conversation.

"Sorry, yes, I'm here."

The sound of her soft, subtle, sexy voice was pure torture on his body. He looked down to see the form of a tent starting where his erection began straining against the inside of his pajama pants. His reaction to her was instantaneous. He was amazed at how the sound of her voice could do this to him.

"I'm sorry. I know I promised right? I didn't mean to make you get quiet on me when I said I was consumed with thoughts of you today."

"It's okay Tyrone. Truth?" she asked as he had done.

"Yes, Victoria, truth," he replied.

"I've been thinking about you as well, all day and evening long. I got in bed tonight with shaky fingers as I dialed your number. I couldn't dial fast enough to talk to you. I know it's bad, but I couldn't help myself either. I guess we're just two hopeless cases," she admitted.

Tyrone laughed.

"I guess we are. If things were different and you were in bed, I would already be on my way to pick you up to come join me here at my house. There would be no need in either of us suffering," he said.

"Suffering is a good word for what this is isn't it?"

"Yes it is," he agreed.

Victoria melted as his smooth voice got softer and a lot deeper as he spoke.

"Tell me now if I'm wrong for telling you how much I miss you and how much I still want you, even with my agreement that I would back off?"

She hesitated knowing they were crossing a line. She didn't want to admit that she was feeling the same way, but she was.

"I want you too Tyrone, but we can't. We can't keep doing this. You know that and I know that," she said, pleading more for her own understanding than for his.

"I know you're right. No matter how much I try I can't seem to stop though. Right this minute, my body is hard just talking to you. If I could control it I would, but I can't," he confessed.

Victoria squirmed around at the mentioning of his hardness. She knew what that meant and she knew what it looked like to see him long, hard and thick waiting for her touch. She closed her eyes at the remembrance of how he felt in her hands, all smooth like silk and hard as steel at the same time. Those thoughts made her moan into the phone and she wished she hadn't. She knew she was loud enough that he'd heard her. He moaned in response to her and when he did, her attempt to keep from touching herself went out the window. She slid her hand under the blanket, touching herself through her panties to try and ease some of the pressure she felt.

"Victoria, baby, you are killing me here with the sounds you're making."

He didn't know what she was doing, but if she was feeling anything like he was he was sure her hands were passing over her body just as he was about to do with his. He reached into his pajama pants to try and ease some of the straining pressure he felt building up. It wasn't the same as having her, but he promised he wouldn't pressure her.

"Victoria," he said softly.

"Yes," she replied on a whisper, already closing her eyes, leaning the phone in the crook of her neck so that she could use both hands to try a little harder for relief.

"What are you doing baby," he said huskily.

"Mmmm," was all she could say.

"I know the feeling," he said. "Are you in the room with the door closed and locked?" he asked.

"Yes, she said throatily. She'd barely gotten that one word out because she was concentrating on the sound of his voice and imagining it was him with his hands between her legs and not her own.

"What are you wearing?" he asked.

"A night shirt and panties," she replied.

"Take off the panties for me, put your hands right where you know I'd have mine if I were there with you."

She didn't hesitate to do as he asked. She removed her panties and tossed the already wet black lace to the floor.

"Tell me Victoria. I want to hear you tell me what you feel."

"Wetness. All I feel is wetness," she said, getting more

and more aroused. The combination of his voice and her fingers were tag teaming her thoughts and her senses.

"Do you remember how I like to make you feel? How I like to touch you?"

"Yes," she said barely able to contain herself. She knew she had to keep her voice down. Even though Duron and Taija's bedroom was far away from hers, she didn't want the quiet of the night to drift the pleasuring sounds emitting from her mouth throughout the house.

"I want you to imagine I'm there with you and that the hand that's rubbing you and the fingers that are about to enter you are mine," he said.

Tyrone was holding himself in his own hand, leaning further back in his chair, gripping himself imagining what Victoria looked like spread out on the bed with her legs open pleasuring herself. The onslaught of the craving for her was bringing him to the brink of climaxing already. He slowed his strokes to prolong the pleasure as long as he could.

When her moaning became more pronounced, he knew that she was driving herself to the edge.

"Not so fast baby, slow it down for me. I need to drag this out for both of us. If I can't be there with you, I want to enjoy it as if I am."

"I'm so hot," she said.

"I know baby, so am I. You always make me feel this way. I'm trying to concentrate on anything other than you spread out like I know you like to do, so that this isn't over too soon," Tyrone said hoarsely, barely able to contain his own release that was slowly creeping up on him again, even with the slower strokes up and down his manhood.

"Can you feel me?" he asked.

"Yes, baby, I feel you. I feel you all over me. I can feel your strong fingers as they tease me over and over. I feel your lips as they grasped one nipple then the other like you enjoyed doing at the hotel," she said while no longer trying to drag out the inevitable.

"I can't hold out any longer, Tyrone," she said as her orgasm slammed into her. She held her breath as she rode out a climax that she seemed to be able to feel in every part of her body. Her body jerked up off of the bed until she had to turn over to scream her release into the pillow to smother the sound.

Even with her face in the pillow and the phone lying next to her face on the pillow where it landed when she turned over, she could also hear Tyrone as he groaned through his own release. Hearing him and the feel of her fingers still stroking her own sensitive nub sent her spiraling into another powerful orgasm. She rode the forever wave hoping it would never end.

Neither spoke as they felt the downward spiral of mutual self-satisfaction.

She knew that this was not the first time she'd pleasured herself to completion with thoughts of him since that first night they had been together. It was even more erotic having him on the phone experiencing it with her.

"Victoria, I think we're in real trouble here baby. No matter how much I agree to backing off, I don't think that's going to work for us," he admitted.

"I know."

"Talk to me, Victoria, about what's going on. Tell me how we can fix this. It's not going away and I'm not sure I can back off like I originally agreed," he said, almost insisting.

"Tyrone, give me some time, okay. Just give me some time."

"Okay, I'll give you some time, but this conversation isn't over. Our one night stand is no longer a one night stand and no matter what, I want more; I want you. I know you feel the same way or we wouldn't be on the phone sticky, needing showers."

"I know. Just give me a little time okay?"

"Okay, I will. Will you call me when you get back to Boston?" he asked.

Victoria knew she shouldn't, but she would be lying if she said no.

"Yes I will."

"Since I know you will, I won't bother you any more while you're here in town. If you want to talk to me, I told you, feel free to call me at any time. I do want you to think about whatever is going on and tell me how I can help. There is no way that you or I can walk away from what's happening between us. Go ahead and get a shower. I look forward to hearing from you when you get to Boston. Sweet dreams, baby," he said before hanging up and getting his own shower. He was messy and happily so.

Chapter 10

Tyrone was back at the office attempting to concentrate on work. Things were quiet with Mike being back on the west coast following his recent wedding to Loren. Tyrone, along with Duron stood as best men at the wedding. He was now sitting at his desk remembering the difference between how he felt being at Duron's wedding and the feelings he felt at Mike's wedding. They were very different.

At Duron's wedding, he didn't have an ounce of jealousy. He was as happy as he could be for his friend because in all the years he'd known him, Duron was happiest that day.

The same was happening with Mike. Tyrone saw him at his happiest and he enjoyed being a part of the day. The difference this time was that he was actually jealous of Mike. Throughout the wedding ceremony, his thoughts kept drifting to Victoria.

Since the night of Taija's baby shower, the few hours they'd spent talking in the park and the hottest night of phone sex of his life with her, they spoke on the phone almost every day since her return to Boston.

They were avoiding talking about the fact that she was still engaged to marry Turner Warfield. Whenever they talked, they spent time learning more and more about each other and not once have either of them brought up the fact that she's still engaged.

Sitting at his desk, he was thinking of picking up the phone to call her. He never called her during the day. It was mostly at night after he was in for the evening. They never talked weddings, engagements or the commitment she was making with Turner soon. They only talked about everyday things and how much they missed each other. There were a few hot nights of phone sex which he really enjoyed, though he wished he could be in bed with her. He loved how she opened up to him and freely engaged in it with him. He especially enjoyed the times when they role-played.

He realized talking to her about little things was also just as enjoyable. He didn't like the feeling that he couldn't proceed forward, nor could he venture backward. He didn't want to go back as if he and Victoria never indulged in intimacy. It bothered him more that he couldn't go forward and have more than a casual friendship with her.

One revelation really stuck to him, but he wouldn't bring that up to her either. He didn't want anything to push her away from him, but so much didn't add up. They spoke on the phone just about every night and sometimes really late, well into the middle of the night. Not one of those nights since Victoria returned to Boston did they speak and Turner was at her place. Every time he called her, she answered. She was always home alone and every night, if he wasn't calling her, she was calling him. He knew for a fact that if Victoria were engaged to him, there would be no way he wouldn't want to spend every night with her, buried deep inside of her, letting her know how much he cared about her and would always want her. What was up with this Turner dude? Why was Victoria doing this to herself?

Perhaps he would find out soon.

He was finally taking the trip to Boston to meet with Turner regarding the business partnership they had spoken about at Taija's shower. Since that night, he and Duron had held a few conference calls with Turner, but now it was time to talk face to face with him and his partners in Boston.

Tyrone would be flying out to Boston in a few days and he didn't know what Victoria was expecting, but he wasn't leaving until they could sit down and have an honest talk about what was going on. There was no way her heart was in this engagement. He could tell from their many conversations that she was just as into him as he was into her and Turner was nowhere in the picture. It angered him that he resorted to playing this game, but whatever was going on was eating away at Victoria and he didn't know how much longer he could go on knowing something wasn't right. She needed to figure it out for herself and Tyrone planned to be around when she did.

~~

Victoria suffered through a very sleepless night. Tyrone was scheduled to fly into Boston to meet with Turner today and that thought made her uneasy. Even though what was going on with she and Turner was a plan, she still didn't want to hurt or embarrass him. A few times since they'd returned to Boston after the baby shower, she thought about telling him about her trip to Texas and her time spent with Tyrone as well as the intimacy they shared while in Atlanta. Each time she thought about clearing the air, she thought of all of the people who would be hurt and she back off. She knew Turner would understand, but what about everyone else who believed in their engagement, she thought to herself.

Turner was her friend. There was a time when she could share anything with him, but they agreed to not date or see anyone until after they divorced a year after the wedding. She knew the agreement was made before she'd hooked up with Tyrone. She just wondered could she go along with the fake wedding, for any reason, and give up on putting serious effort behind being involved openly with Tyrone.

She'd just arrived at the office and after the third or fourth yawn, she realized she needed coffee to get focused.

She grabbed her coffee and headed back to her office just in time to grab her ringing office phone. It was Turner.

"Hey Turner, what's up?" she asked.

"Not much. Tyrone Davis from Pioneer Architecture & Design is coming in for a meeting this afternoon. He should have landed already even though the meeting isn't until two this afternoon."

Victoria didn't want to tell him that he didn't need to let her know. She knew all about Tyrone's visit to Boston.

"I forgot about that," she lied.

"I was calling to see if you wanted to go with me tonight to take Tyrone out for dinner? I thought after the meeting later, that we could have some down time and enjoy an evening where we weren't talking about work."

The thought had Victoria's nerves on edge. Could she really sit at a table across from Tyrone and her growing feelings and deep desire for him not show? She didn't want to take the risk.

"No, you go ahead. I have a lot of work to catch up on. Go ahead and take him to dinner and call me later to let me know how everything as far as the business collaboration worked out," she said, hoping he wouldn't press her.

"Okay, I'll talk to you later then."

Victoria was happy because she knew she wouldn't have survived the dinner. She did have hope that even though he was in town, that he would at least give her a call. She looked forward to his calls and when she felt like talking to him earlier some evenings, she would call him and they would talk for hours.

What are you doing? Victoria said to herself. This wasn't the first time she had questioned herself.

She was engaged to marry one man, unreal as it was, and falling hard for another. She wondered how much longer she could keep this up. Her nerves were on edge as she thought about Tyrone being on her home turf. She knew it would be very easy to see him before he returned to Atlanta. Her body was screaming yes, but her level head was telling her to forget about it by busying herself with work until he left. She had to do that in order to keep her sanity and her panties intact.

~~

Victoria had been home for a few hours waiting for a call from either Tyrone or Turner. She had no doubt the business end went well. She was more concerned with the down time conversation. After getting her shower and climbing into bed, her cell phone rang. Looking at it, her heart skipped a beat when she saw that it was Tyrone.

"Hi, Victoria," he said in that voice that excited her every time she heard it.

"I was hoping you would call," she said, unashamed at her instant desire for him. It was now far beyond her control. Just hearing his voice did things to her psyche as well as sensitive parts of her body.

"Your wish is my command sweetheart," he said. "You know I aim to please."

"Yes I do. How did things go with the meeting?" she asked while turning out her lamp and snuggling further down in her bed. She loved talking to him in the dark of night with the only light being cast, coming from the high moon outside of her window.

"Extremely well. I think we'll definitely be in business together. Turner seems to really know what he wants and his ideas for expanding his family's business are incredible. We're looking forward to helping him carry out his dreams. Later in the year I'm hoping to take a trip to Washington to see the winery and vineyards. The pictures, though incredible, I'm sure they don't do it justice."

He paused before speaking again.

"Turner also appears to be a good guy Victoria. I know we talk everyday about everything we can think of except the elephant in the room, but sooner or later we need to address this. I'm finding myself falling hard for you and I don't share. Tell me how you feel about me, baby. I need to know and I need to know tonight," he said, almost pleading.

It was a plea that she felt deep down in her spirit.

"I care about you a great deal too. I just have some things to work out and all I can do is ask you to be patient with me, please. Just be a little more patient with me and let me work this out," she said, hoping he cared enough about her to let her do this.

Tyrone could hear the struggle in her voice. He knew that whatever was going on was causing her a lot of pain and all he could hope was that soon, she would tell him what was going on. Clearly she and Turner were not really in love. He knew it because he watched Turner as he made eye contact with a specific woman throughout the dinner and drinks they shared after the meeting. It was a woman who clearly was into him and he was into her, but they were playing it very coy. The way Turner had been in tuned to the mystery woman is what he expected to see when he saw Victoria and Turner together. It was the kind of look he had every time he saw Victoria. Turner tried to hide his interest in the mystery woman, but Tyrone caught him ogling her. She was a very beautiful and exotic looking woman that any man would be lucky to be with and just like Turner had for her, the woman only had eyes for him.

He didn't want to be the one to tell Victoria what he witnessed while out with Turner. He didn't want to cause her any more grief. He would give her the space to work it out, but in the meantime, he had no plans to back out on her either. He knew she was well worth the wait and he was a very patient man.

Victoria noticed that the air seemed to crackle around her. Everything was quiet yet intense at the same time. Tyrone had to notice it as well because his deep voice spoke to her and when he did, the blanket covering her body and the nightie she had on felt like unnecessary weight. Even though the house was a little chilly, she felt on fire.

"Victoria, can I change the tone of our nightly

conversation a bit?" he asked.

"Yes," was all she could utter.

"Would you like to know what I'm doing right this very moment?"

"Yes," she whispered, hoping it as something naughty.

"I'm sitting in my hotel suite still fully clothed in my suit, talking to you and before I knew what was happening, the minute I heard your voice, my body got extremely hard at the thought of you. I couldn't help myself when my trousers felt like a prison to what was straining behind my zipper. I found myself unzipping my pants and reaching inside to find a way to relieve the tension, the strain and the stress of not being able to have you right now."

Victoria's body was already on the verge of shooting off like a rocket, just from his voice and the words he was saying.

"Do you know what I was thinking before I called you?" he asked.

"No," she said softly.

"I was wondering if while I'm talking to you, you would be so turned on that you would reached into your nightstand or wherever you keep your toys and pleasure yourself thinking about me being in Boston close enough to touch unlike when I'm back home in Atlanta and can only reach out over the phone. Are you a toy kind of woman, baby?" he asked, already knowing the answer. Of course she was. There was no way a woman as sexual as she was would not have a few laying around for those nights when a man just wouldn't do.

"Victoria, baby, can you hear me? Are you listening?"

"Yes I hear you," she said, barely able to concentrate. She was too turned on to focus.

"Well?" he continued to prod.

"Yes I am," she admitted.

"Do you have one nearby?" he asked really getting excited now.

"Yes."

"Get it and turn it on. I want to hear it," he said.

Victoria's hands were shaking, she was so stimulated as she reached in her night table for one of her favorite ones.

"Do you have it?" he asked.

"Yes," she said turning it on.

"Oh, it must be a big one because the sound is extremely loud," he said, knowing the pleasure they would both soon experience as he listened to her through the phone with what was a poor substitution for him, but what would certainly do under the circumstance.

"Let me hear you baby. Don't hold anything back," he said almost choking to get his words out.

Tyrone put his cell on speaker phone and placed it on the table in front of him. He placed it close enough to him so that he could hear her every sigh and squeal of pleasure.

It wasn't until she called out his name when she climaxed that he ventured over the edge with her. His orgasm seemed to go on without stopping as he listened to her ride out her pleasure on a toy that he wanted to be in place of.

He was glad that they could easily fall into phone sex without hesitation, but it only made him want her more. If it wasn't for the fact that he was in Boston, he knew that being with her would be an impossibility, but here he was. Not far from her at all.

"Victoria, baby, are you alright over there?" he asked when he could once again speak.

"Yes. I have never felt so much pleasure from this thing before. I mean it always does the trick, but never, ever like tonight with you on the phone and never so fast," she exclaimed.

"I need to see you Victoria. Can I come over?" he asked, full of hope.

Tyrone knew that she could hear him, but whether she was listening or not was another story. He could only imagine what she was doing to her own body right now because he could still hear the toy humming through the phone. She hadn't turned it off.

"Victoria? I need to see you. I know we agreed to stay away from each other, but I can't stay away. Not when I'm in the same city that you're in and only a car drive away. I'll understand if you tell me you're expecting company, but if not, I really need to see you. Tell me I can come over. I can tell you need this as much as I do. You know you can't stay away from me any more than I can stay away from you."

He hoped this wasn't a night that she was expecting Turner. From the looks of things when he'd left Turner at the restaurant, he appeared to have other plans in the form of the sexy number he exchanged looks with all evening.

He tried to wait patiently for her to reply. He could still hear her moaning through the phone. He needed to be inside of her.

"Victoria, come on baby, answer me?"

Tyrone got his answer when Victoria read him her address over the phone and hung up.

Chapter 11

Turner waited outside of the restaurant in his car for Cecily where he and Tyrone ate earlier for dinner. He wasn't expecting to see her tonight. He couldn't help but stare the moment she entered with her friends. He could tell that she was about to come over to his table until he signaled to her that he wasn't alone. She understood and backed off, going in the direction of her table with her friends.

He was in a dilemma. He'd recently met Cecily at a business meeting to discuss his engagement to Victoria. It was the day they sat for photos and interviews that would later be broadcasted nationally. She was the reporter who was interviewing them regarding his taking over his family's winery and vineyard soon and even asking where he and Victoria were going for their honeymoon. They shared an instant attraction despite the fact that they discussed his engagement and pending marriage. For the first time in his life, he'd met a woman who took his breath away and not just because she was lovely. The same night of the interview, they'd met up and gone back to his house and made love in every room until the sun came up in the morning. That night, he shared with her that he'd never felt such an attraction to any woman before. They stayed up all night talking and couldn't believe how much they had in common.

Turner took a risk and shared with Cecily that his marriage to Victoria was a fake. He really wanted Cecily, but right now he was in a bind because he and Victoria had an agreement. What was a man to do when he met the woman of his dreams and it through a wrench in the plans he had for his immediate future? he thought to himself.

He looked up at the restaurant entrance at the very moment Cecily exited, looking around for him. He flashed his lights letting her know where he was. He watched the woman, who was now the love of his life, head in his direction. She was going to help him figure out a way to have the necessary talk with Victoria that he knew he needed to have. He needed to break off the engagement so that he could marry Cecily. Turner exited his car as soon as she reached it and before he could prepare, she leaped into his arms. He inhaled her scent, something he was getting used to and didn't want to live without.

"Hi love," he said.

"Hi back," she replied.

He didn't waste any time saying what burned in his mind all evening.

"I think it's time, baby. I need to talk to Victoria and I need to do it soon. I didn't realize until tonight when you walked in the restaurant and you had to halt coming over to me that I couldn't do this anymore. I didn't like having to do that and I never want to do it again," he said with a passion filled voice.

"I love you, Turner. I will support whatever you want to

do and when you want to do it. I know it's going to be hard, but I believe if Victoria is the person you have been telling me she is, she will understand and your friendship won't be in jeopardy. I look forward to this all working out and us all being the best of friends," Cecily said, reassuring him and believing every word she'd just said.

"You're right. I'll go and talk to her tomorrow night. I think this would have been easier if the story of my engagement had not already made it to the media. I'll have a lot of explaining to do to my family along with apologies, but first Victoria is owed an explanation and an apology. I love you and I can't wait to marry you," he said as they got in his car to go to her place where he would devour her all night long.

~~

Victoria stood in her living room pacing back and forth waiting for Tyrone to get to her. She didn't hesitate when the chance came for her to see him before he went back to Atlanta. She may be fighting her true feelings because of the circumstances, but she knew without a shadow of a doubt she was in love with him and she needed to see and touch him like she needed her next breath.

Excitement shot through her body when she saw bright lights shine through her front window signally Tyrone had pulled into her driveway.

The excitement over him actually being at her house was so overpowering that she couldn't wait for him to get to the door. She swung the front door open and ran to meet him at the car.

It's a good thing Tyrone had a minute to prepare for Victoria's launch at him. He had a split second to brace himself as she leaped into his arms, wrapping her arms around his neck and her legs around his waist. He didn't realize how much he needed this until now. As she showered his face with kiss after kiss, he walked with her in his arms toward her house. He didn't want to give the neighbors a show of everything he was about to do to her.

When they were inside with the door locked, he wasted no time asking her in what direction he should go to get to her room.

Once there, he laid her down on the bed while he shrugged out of his clothes. Once he had divested himself of every piece of clothing, he joined her on the bed.

"I have dreamed of being in bed with you again, not that I didn't enjoy our escapade against the wall in Duron's house or our many erotic phone sex sessions, but nothing compares to being here with you again, on a soft bed with all of your soft parts thrashing around under me," he said before leaning down and kissing her with a kiss that was filled with warmth, tenderness and seduction. As his tongue assaulted her mouth, he let his hands wander all over her exquisite body, acclimating himself to her once again.

"You are perfect, Victoria. I want to be sure I tell you that and that you know I mean every word of it. You are perfect, baby."

Before she could respond, he kissed her again, stealing her words with his lips. He continued kissing her while his hands reached up to unclasp the front closure of the nightie she was wearing. He had no idea that she was in this frilly thing when she ran into his arms covered in a soft, plush robe.

Once he unsnapped and unhooked the closures, he only untied the tiny ribbon that held the two sides together and the garment fell away from her body. He remembered telling her the first night that they were together that he loved high-cut, lacey panties on a woman and she wowed him tonight with a sheer lacey pink pair that matched the nightie.

He was surprised the bed didn't burst into flames as hot as he was for her.

After he had the garment off, he slid his hand down, while still enjoying the response to his kiss Victoria was putting on him, and removed the lacey material from her shapely hips.

She lifted so that he could rid her of her panties and when she was again relaxed against the bed, she reached out for that part of him that could never be replaced by an electric vibrating adult toy.

"That toy did the trick with you on the phone, but I prefer the real thing over that piece of plastic any day," she said while stroking the length of him, eliciting a sound from him that said that he was already very close.

He loved the feel of her hand stroking him again, but he needed to stop her before he spilled his seed all over her, ending what he was hoping would be an entire night of lovemaking.

He reached for her hand to stop her strokes.

"Baby, I love how your hand feels and any other time, I would let you continue until you wanted to stop, but I'm not sure I can take any more. I want to be sure that I'm inside of you when the explosion happens. I need to feel you wrapped tightly around me, milking me for every bit of pleasure you need. I want incredible memories of you when I have to return home to Atlanta."

They continued to kiss while he reached for the condom

packet he'd placed on the bed when he entered her bedroom. A mere second after putting it on, he entered her body in one long plunged.

"I've missed you," he said. "I've missed this," he added, talking about being seated deep in her body.

"I've missed you too, so much," she said in response.

She meant every word of it too. Being with Tyrone felt like heaven. It wasn't solely because the sex was good, but because he was turning out to be the man she had longed for all of her life. The connection they shared was one that she'd never known with a man before and she only wanted this feeling with him. She couldn't think right now about her situation with Turner. It wasn't what she wanted or needed it to be. It was what it was. Tyrone on the other hand was what she wanted and needed.

She was happy just to be able to feel his naked body against hers once again.

She closed her eyes and felt delight at how good he was making her feel.

"Look at me baby. Look at me and tell me how you want it. This night is for you," he said, slowing his strokes in and out of her body and watching the play of emotions that crossed her face, telling him just how much she was already enjoying his invasion in her body.

Her womanhood was holding on to him like a vice grip as if she planned to never let him leave her body again. He loved the feeling of her muscles to gripping him tighter on each passage in and out of her body.

"Baby, you are so hard, I think I can feel the veins that protrude when you are highly aroused and span the length of you. You feel so good," she mumbled.

"I need it slow, but hard and deep," she replied, setting

the pace for how she wanted him to move inside of her. She wanted to feel every single stroke. Like him, she needed lasting memories when he had to return home.

Tyrone changed his stroke so that it was just how she wanted it. Her pleasure filled sigh gave him the answer that he was right on point.

To add to the pleasure, when she closed her eyes to concentrate on the feeling, he reached down to pull her legs up higher around his waist so that his strokes would be even deeper. He slid his hands slowly up her sides and gripped her hands, entwining them with his own. As they continued with their rocking motion, he took one of her hands and placed her middle finger in his mouth, imitating the motion of how her body was gripping his penis like it belonged to her and only her.

The jolt of the feeling of her finger inside of Tyrone's mouth drove her to forget about the slow motion she wanted him to go in and she increased the paced. She didn't know her fingers could tingle the way they were doing inside of his mouth. She could feel it in her breast as the sensation traveled throughout her body. She continued her upward thrusts, going faster and faster and he obliged her by keeping up with the pace he was letting her set. She was witnessing the most erotic scene ever, watching as Tyrone sucked her finger in and out of his mouth.

"That's it baby, get it. Take all of me. I'm yours and you're mine. Do you hear me, Victoria," he asked as he watched an orgasm first cross her face before shattering her body into pieces.

"You're mine," he said, finding his own release, throwing his head back and releasing a growl that would have all of the animals in the neighborhood barking if they could hear him.

"I have no control when it comes to you and I like it," he said while kissing the sweat from her face. He loved being with her like this and he didn't want to extricate himself from her body. He wanted to stay in this exact position forever, never being separated from her again.

As their breathing returned to normal, the reality of the situation also returned to normal. She was still engaged to another man and he would soon be returning to Atlanta, leaving her in Boston with her fiancé. It pained him to think that she was sharing her body with him.

Somewhere deep in his mind he felt that he was the only one making love to her. That thought brought him joy and he only hoped he was correct. He couldn't imagine her responding to any other man the way she responded to him.

When he made an attempt to move and Victoria gripped him around his neck to pull him closer to her body, keeping him from doing so, he pulled her tighter to him understanding. They would probably never be able to have a moment like this again and she wanted to hold on to the feeling as much as he did.

"No don't move. I love how you feel right now and I don't want to lose this feeling," she said with a voice that made Tyrone think that she was about to cry.

Now he felt bad. He knew her words weren't because of regret or guilt, but because she was feeling about him the same way he was feeling about her.

The feelings he was developing for her were new to him. He didn't want to be without her. He didn't want to leave to return home without her. He wanted to stay right where he was and never leave, never giving up the way he was feeling at the moment. He needed to help her work through whatever was going on.

"Victoria, baby, listen," he said in her ear while still locked inside of her body. As he spoke, he could feel her body start to shake from the crying she could no longer contain. He did remove himself from her body, against her protest so that they could talk.

He rolled over and pulled her on top of him so that he could look right into her eyes.

"Tell me what you need. We can't continue like this, so tell me what you need and I'll do my best to give it to you, whatever it is. What we have been developing is rare sweetheart," he said reaching up to wipe away the tears that were continuing to stream down her face.

"This isn't some fluke that we just fell into a pattern of hitting the sheets when we see each other. All of our nights of talking, getting to know each other and discovering we have so many things in common is what most couples dream of having. Here we have it and we can't be together. I'm not trying to ruin any plans you have for your life. I just know that what we have is not fly by night; it's real and true and I don't want to have to keep walking away from it. I don't want to have to keep walking away from you. Tell me why you're crying? Is this a good or a bad cry? Are you regretting that I came over? Was this too much?"

Tyrone waited for some type of response from her. He watched her try to gather her words through the tears.

"No one," she said while talking through her tears, "has ever made me feel the way you do. I'm not just talking about intimacy either. I feel so comfortable and free when I'm talking to you and I feel like I can tell you any and everything. It feels like you are the half of me that I've been missing and have been longing for."

Victoria opened her eyes and noticed that Tyrone looked confused. She assumed he was thinking about Turner and what her feelings were for him.

"I don't want to bring up Turner with you and I lying here naked in my bed, but just know that what I feel for him is not what I feel for you. It doesn't compare. I can't explain it right now, but I want you to know that I am so happy when I'm with you and when I talk to you. This situation is just overwhelming and I'm confused about what to do," she said crying harder. "I want to be with you so bad I ache for you."

He didn't like seeing her this way. She was deeply bothered by whatever was going on that he wasn't privy to. He didn't come to her tonight for this. He came for mutual comfort and instead, his presence was upsetting her. He didn't want that. Whatever was going on with Turner it seemed like she was carrying the weight of the world on her shoulders. They would talk but tonight wasn't the night. He wanted to give her time to calm down. He didn't want to spend his only night with her crying and confused.

He pulled her back down so that she was snuggling with him, side by side on the bed.

"Let's not talk about this right now. I came here because I wanted to make you feel good, not make you perplexed about your situation. Calm down, baby," he said, soothing her by rubbing up and down her back to comfort her.

"I'm sorry for crying all over you."

"No more talk, no more pressure," he said. "I came here to be with you, so let me do that," he added, when he pulled her close to him and kissed her passionately while pulling her under him at the same time to remove any sad feelings from her mind and replacing them with only thoughts of how good they were together. He kissed her with all of the passion he could pour into her and when she began responding to him with enthusiasm, he wanted to kiss and love her misery away. He had no plans to waste the night worrying about tomorrow when he could use the time to focus on the two of them tonight.

~~

Tyrone came awake slowly and reached for Victoria only to discover she was no longer in bed with him. He realized it was still dark outside so it wasn't quite morning yet. He got up, slipped on his trousers and went in search of her. He was saddened to see Victoria standing at the bay window in her living in her robe looking out with a sad look on her face.

He walked up behind her, bringing her back against him as he pulled her protectively into his arms.

"What's wrong Victoria?" he asked.

She hesitated before responding. She wanted to be totally honest with him. There was enough pretending in the situation already.

"I love you, Tyrone. I am in love with you and I don't know what to do about it."

He was happy to hear those words come from her mouth. He knew he was in love with her, but given her situation with Turner, he felt she didn't need the extra added pressure. He was surprised that the word love didn't scare him as much as he thought it would. He was actually feeling the same way about her too and he didn't care who she was engaged to.

"I love you too, baby. This whole situation is crazy, but I do love you too. It hurts me that I can't have you. I don't understand why. Do you love Turner?"

"Not like you think. I do, but nothing like what I feel when I think of you."

Tyrone's confusion now went to another level. He turned her around to face him.

"Are you ready to tell me what's going on here? You can't be in love with two men," he said with a little more anger than he wanted her to see. This was ridiculous. To him the solution was clear. She needed to break off her engagement with Turner and give her all to being with Tyrone.

Victoria knew what he wanted, but she couldn't it to him. She knew he was thinking that it was time for her to break things off with Turner and be happy with him. As much as Victoria wanted to, she couldn't.

"I can't talk about this right now. I just can't and I'm sorry if you don't understand that, but I just can't."

He pulled away from her, now getting frustrated.

"Aren't you tired of apologizing to me for not doing what's in your heart? There is clearly something not on the up and up here with you and Turner. I sensed it from the start when I first saw you two together in Atlanta. I'm here with you now and I know something isn't right. Love is supposed to make you happy, not sad. You obviously are not happy in this relationship with Turner. If that's the case, then break it off. I'm not saying it because I want you; I'm saying it because you love me and I love you. That should be incentive enough. You can't continue like this. It's tearing you up inside baby."

He backed up from her so that they could see each other clearly using the moon in the sky as light.

"Victoria, I know you're engaged to Turner, so this may

be a crazy question, but I need to know the answer."

"Okay," she responded, waiting for the question.

"Are you sleeping with Turner also?"

His question was unexpected and her heart raced at the thought of how to answer. She knew the answer, but wasn't sure if she should share it because it would cause more questions than it would answer. She also knew she couldn't look in the face of the man she loved and lie to him about that. If nothing else, she needed him to know that she wasn't sharing her body with another man."

"No, Tyrone, I'm not sleeping with Turner."

He was happy to hear that, but that only led to more questions in his mind.

"Okay, let me try this since we're on a roll here. Have you ever had sex with Turner?" he said, feeling like he knew the answer, but needed to hear it from her.

She looked down at the carpet before she felt Tyrone's fingers lift her chin back up so that when she responded, she was looking right at him.

"Don't look away from me baby. Look at me and tell me," he said.

"No, I've never had sex with Turner," she disclosed and waited while the shock of what she'd just said registered with him.

Tyrone was losing patience.

"Let me see if I have this correct. You're engaged to a man you've never been intimate with. I wouldn't really find a problem with that if I thought that it was because you were a virgin or someone simply waiting to have sex with your fiancé until you got married, abstaining, but clearly that's not the case since you're obviously not abstaining, so what gives?" he asked, almost pleading with her to shed light on everything.

"I can't tell you that."

He didn't wait for her to continue with not being able to come clean with him.

"How long have you known Turner?" he asked.

"All my life," she answered without pause.

"So this is someone you've known all your life, who you aren't in love with, who you haven't been intimate with, but who you plan to marry sometime in the near future. Is that about right?" he asked, clearly upset now.

Victoria could see that he was just about through with her. His anger was about to boil over. Everything was baffling and though she could very well clear things up, she still owed Turner her trust. As much as she wanted to get out of the commitment she made to him in agreeing to marry him, she couldn't do it. He would stand to lose so much if she backed out now and she couldn't do that to him. Not even for the love of the man of her dreams.

She moved closer to him with hopes of explaining some kind of way and she was crushed when he suddenly took more steps backwards away from her.

"Don't," he said. "Unless you are ready to tell me what's going on, don't. Do you still plan to marry Turner?" he asked, hoping that her answer would be no.

He waited, holding his breath for her answer.

"Victoria? You just told me you loved me. I told you I loved you. You also told me you aren't in love with Turner and you share no intimacy. My question again is, do you still plan to marry him?"

She knew her next statement was going to hurt, but she had to get it out.

"Yes, Tyrone. I still plan to marry Turner."

Tyrone was incensed hearing her say she still planned to marry a man she didn't love. None of this sounded normal and clearly they were not on the same page. He didn't know what else to say. After all they'd just shared, she was still planning to marry another man. Nothing about this made any sense to him.

Victoria watches as emotions similar to rage, impatience and misunderstanding crossed Tyrone's face and she was more sorry than she'd ever been in her life for making him feel this way. She didn't mean to hurt him, but she couldn't figure out a way to make him understand without telling him everything and she couldn't do that. She started to speak again when Tyrone made a sudden move in the direction of the stairs.

"I think it's time for me to leave," he said, turning to get his clothes. He heard her calling out to him, but he didn't stop until he reached the bedroom. He searched frantically for his clothes and rushed to get them on. He didn't know what he was doing here. He set himself up for this. He knew she was engaged to someone else and now that he knew that she loved him and he loved her, things were clear with how they should proceed. Why the hell was she still marrying a man she didn't love? What was it with women? he thought to himself. He did the one thing he said he never wanted to do and that was fall in love because deep down, he had a feeling it wouldn't turn out well for him. Victoria's actions proved he was right in the way he felt. Women couldn't be trusted and they were about lying and scheming. She had no problem sharing her body or her heart with him, but she was will to share her life with someone else. As he continued to dress, he wondered to himself how he could allow himself to be drawn into a woman's web. He'd avoided traps like this by not getting serious with anyone.

His mother tried trapping a man with a baby because she loved him, but he didn't love or want her, yet she continued on with her plan. Even after she delivered Tyrone, she continued to play games to get him to leave his wife. When that didn't work, she thought that she would tell him that she was willing to give up the baby if he didn't want him if she thought they could be together. When that didn't work, she left him anyway. What was it that made women make terrible life decisions instead of following what was logical and true?

He stood in Victoria's face and told her he was in love with her too and yet it didn't convince her to break things off with Turner. He was an idiot for thinking he could find love and happiness for himself. Apparently it wasn't meant to be or in the cards for him. Reality had him seeing all of this was a mistake. Just like he was stupid all those years hoping his mother would come to her senses and realize that he should have been the first priority to her, he'd put trust in another woman only to be let down. Like his mother, Victoria didn't know what was good for her either. He'd had enough. He wouldn't continue to put his heart on the line for a woman who clearly didn't have a clue what she wanted.

Now completely dressed, he went back downstairs to see Victoria standing at the closed front door.

"Tyrone, don't leave like this, please," she pleaded.

"I'm not leaving because I want to. I'm leaving because I have to. This is not a healthy situation for either one of us. You obviously have struggles you need to work out and I need to walk away. I don't see a win situation here and that's sad. I don't know what I was thinking getting caught up in this with a woman who wears another man's ring."

He looked down and noticed she no longer had the ring on.

"When did you take your ring off?" he asked her.

Victoria didn't answer. She put her hands behind her back, knowing it was too late to hide the obvious. She'd taken it off the moment she'd come in from work. Her removing it had nothing to do with Tyrone. She took it off every day once she was home and out of the public eye.

"Too late sweetheart. I already saw that you're not wearing it."

"Tyrone, I didn't take it off to be deceitful because you were coming over. I take it off every day once I'm home for the evening."

"Why?" he asked, then thought about what the answer could be and realized he didn't want to know.

"Forget that I asked that. I don't even want to know. The ring is the smallest issue in all of this. What we have, I've never had with any other woman before. I believe that we have something beautiful here. You obviously don't think so. I thought I could deal with this because I could continue to have a piece of you, but a piece of you is not enough anymore. Now that I know you love me and you know that I love you, I don't think either one of us should have to settle for anything other than an open and honest relationship."

He watched for any change in her facial expression, but saw nothing.

"Tyrone I'm sorry baby. I do love you and I wish I could explain, but I can't right now. I promise you I will and soon. I need to think things through," she pleaded.

He no longer wanted to give her time to think. It was clear that coming to her was a huge mistake. He knew asking her any questions was something he wished he could take back. He now knew more than he wanted.

"I'll tell you what, I'll let you figure it out. I hope you and Turner will be very happy, though I doubt it. I will be just fine. I don't want to keep doing this sneaking around like a couple of teenagers. We're grown and in control of our actions and our faculties. It's obvious it's not love you want because it's about to walk out the door. Please move away from the door," he said, not being able to look her in the face as he spoke. It hurt him to see her break down in tears as she moved away from the door so that he could leave, but if he couldn't get her to see that she was making a mistake then his leaving was the right decision for him and her.

"Tyrone, I love you," she said as he opened the door to leave.

"You can't possibly love me if you still plan to marry another man, whatever the reason may be."

That was the last thing Victoria heard him say before he got in his car and drove off. She finally shut and locked the door and slid down to the floor in a pool of tears as realization set in. She'd just lost the man of her dreams, the love of her life.

Chapter 12

Things worked out well for Tyrone on the business front with this trip, but personally it had turned out poorly. On the drive back to the hotel he played the conversation over and over again in his head and couldn't figure out how things had gone so wrong with Victoria. Even though he'd never been in love before, he was sure it wasn't supposed to make him feel as bad as it did.

His flight wasn't scheduled to leave out until the afternoon, but he wanted to get to the airport and be ready to leave as soon as the plane was ready to take off. He didn't have a reason for staying any longer than he needed to at the hotel or in Boston. He needed to get back to Atlanta and put this trip behind him.

He did have a lot to talk about with Duron and Mike regarding the business deal with Turner that would be beneficial to them all. No matter what was happening on a personal level, the project with Turner was going to be huge.

He gathered his things together, checked out of the hotel and headed for the airport. It was now a little after six in the morning and he still had about five hours before his flight out.

The hotel where he was staying was nice and in the middle of a very nice residential area. He exited the hotel garage and made a turn to check out some of the historical houses in the area. He'd been to Boston several times before, but never to the area that he was currently in. He drove around a few of the blocks checking out the historic nature when he gave a couple standing on the steps of a brownstone lip locking a second look. He knew the guy without a doubt. It was Turner, Victoria's fiancé. He sat watching them as they practically devoured each other. They clearly had spent the night together and when he saw that Turner finally came up for air, he also recognized the woman. It was the same woman Turner had eyed at the restaurant the evening before. Apparently Victoria wasn't the only one of the two of the holding secrets.

He noticed that Turner was still in the same suit from the night before as the woman was trying her best to hold her robe together in the brisk wind that was blowing. The car horn behind him startled him out of his trance and he drove off.

This is some crazy mess, he thought. It was clear that neither Turner nor Victoria were abstaining from sex before the wedding and what was even more clear was the fact that they weren't engaging in it with each other. For the first time since he'd first ran into Victoria in Texas, he wished he hadn't. He now found himself caught up in a woman who loved him, but was marrying another man who was also seeing another woman. This was the sort of stuff people read about in books and magazines.

As he drove on to the airport he still couldn't believe

Victoria was willing to give up what they shared and what they could have to marry a man she didn't love and who obviously didn't love her either. He wished she would talk to him instead of letting him leave without laying it all out so that they could find a way to fix it. For now, this wasn't a situation for him and he needed to go home and forget about her.

~~

It had been hours since Tyrone had left and she was still sitting on the floor with her back to the front door. She couldn't get up the strength to move. Her life was turned upside down and she didn't know how to fix it. What should have been memories of an unforgettable night of lovemaking with Tyrone had turned into an ending she didn't want.

She originally stayed seated at the door hoping he would turn around, come back and tell her he loved her enough to give her time to work out what she needed to do. Her mind was cloudy with her love for him and her commitment to Turner and knowing he wanted an explanation right away had put her in a bind. She wanted to tell him everything, but she needed to think through the ramifications of doing so.

Now that it had been a few hours since he'd left, she knew he wasn't coming back and she needed to pick herself up and deal with the reality of the day. Her first desire was to pick up the phone and call Taija in hopes that through their close friendship, she could help soothe a broken heart and give her advice on what to do. She knew that wasn't a possibility because not only had she not come clean with Tyrone, she hadn't with Taija either so confiding in her wasn't a possibility. She had no one and in the stillness of the morning, she felt like she had no one.

She didn't know what to do next. All she knew was that she let the man she loved walk away thinking she didn't want him and that was the furthest thing from the truth.

She headed for the steps to her bedroom and when she saw the ruffled sheets, the impact of her decision to leave Tyrone in the dark hit her full force. She would never be able to get in her bed again and not think of making love with him. Another reality also hit her suddenly; Tyrone had proclaimed his love for her. She knew a lot about him from Taija and she knew that there was never a shortage of women in his life and he could have any woman he wanted. She also knew that he'd never been in a relationship before, preferring the single, player life instead.

'How could I have done this?' she said to herself. She had hurt the man who had never before told a woman he loved her and she should have been happy knowing that if he said it, he really meant it because it would not have come easy for him to say. The full weight of how things ended with Tyrone came over her and she crawled into her bed, grabbed the pillow he'd slept on which still held his scent and she cried herself to sleep.

~~

Tyrone settled into the business lounge at the airport waiting the last hour for his flight to take off. As much as he tried to focus on work, he couldn't take his mind off of everything that occurred during his stay in Boston. He was already missing Victoria, but he knew he couldn't continue on the path they were going on. His phone rang and thinking it may be Victoria, he was planning to not answer it because he wasn't ready to talk to her. Instead it was his grandmother. She rarely called him when she knew he was away on business and he'd told her he would be in Boston.

"Gram, hi," he said. "Is everything alright?"

"Yes son, it is. Do you realize you ask me that every time I call you," she laughed.

"Sorry Gram. You know how much I worry about you. I wish you would move to Atlanta so that I wouldn't have to worry about you so much. You know I can take care of you if you did."

"Son, I don't want to have that conversation with you again. I like my life just fine here in Texas. If you get a wife and some grandbabies for me one day, I might think about it."

Tyrone knew that wasn't going to happen so he let it go.

"I hear you loud and clear, Gram. I won't ask you about moving and you won't ask me about a wife and grandchildren," he laughed.

"Good. I was calling to say hello and to also tell you that your mother stopped by here today for a visit."

He didn't know how to respond. He felt some kind of way about his mother and it wasn't a good way.

"Aren't you going to ask me anything about her?" she pressed.

"No, I'm not. You know I don't want to talk about her."

"I know son, but she wants to see you. She said she saw you in a magazine or something and was real proud of you and was hoping that the two of you could talk and possibly start over."

"Start over? Gram, come on. I'm a grown man. She left when I was a little boy. She could have come around at any time and she chose not to. I don't want to discuss her and I definitely don't want to see her."

"Okay son. I didn't mean to upset you," she said.

Tyrone knew he was being more abrasive than he needed to be, especially with his grandmother, but with all that had happened with Victoria and now more drama with his mother, he wasn't having a good day.

"Gram, I love you. You could never upset me. I'm just not having a good day."

"What's the matter Tyrone? Is there anything you want to talk about?"

"No, I'll work my way through it. If everything is okay, I'm in an airport in Boston and my flight is about to board. I'll call you when I get back home."

"Okay son. I love you and I'll talk to you soon."

After disconnecting with his grandmother, he thought what more could possibly go wrong with this day.

Chapter 13

A week had passed and Victoria was so accustomed to talking to Tyrone and that being the bright spot of her day that she couldn't seem to focus since he'd returned to Atlanta after the trip to Boston. She missed him, but understood when he didn't pick up when she called or returned any of the messages she'd left on his voicemail. She knew he needed space from her and she knew she should let him have it, but she missed him terribly. She had no right still calling or asking him to forgive her. What she was doing was unforgiveable and she'd hurt him. She looked in his face and told him she loved him, but she would still be marrying another man. She has never been in a predicament like the one she was in now.

She walked into her office to see Turner sitting on the sofa, looking relaxed. He smiled when she entered, then turned that smile into a frown when he saw that she didn't seem to be happy to see him. Work kept him busy all week and he hadn't had a chance to talk to her. He wanted to have a heart to heart with her and tell her about Cecily, but sensed this wasn't the time to do so.

"Hey Victoria. Is everything alright with you? You seem a little out of sorts today," he said, getting up and coming to sit in the chair right in front of her desk after she'd taken a seat behind it.

"I'm fine Turner. You know me, a crazy work week. I'm surprised to see you here today and so early in the morning."

"I know, I was hoping we could talk, but maybe we can do it later. Your mind seems to be clouded today. Anything I can help with?" he asked.

She wished it was that simple. She wished that she could tell him that she was in love with Tyrone and couldn't fulfill her promise to marry him and that she was sorry if he was going to lose everything, but she couldn't marry him. That's what she wanted to say and then maybe she could get some semblance of normalcy back in her life. That's not what she did though. She'd thought about it all week and had not come up with a way to break the news to him. The longer she didn't hear from Tyrone, the more she thought that maybe she would just go ahead with the original plan. There was no hope for her and Tyrone now so marrying Turner would not be a problem, except that it was. She wanted to be with Tyrone. She wanted love and passion. She wanted to go to bed and wake up every single morning with Tyrone next to her. She wanted him; she needed him. How did she get herself in such a mess, she thought.

"No, it's something I need to work through on my own, but thanks for always looking out for me," she said.

"Okay, well I stopped by because I haven't seen you all week and I wanted to check on you and perhaps talk. Since you are preoccupied, we can do this another time."

"Thanks Turner, that would be great. I have a meeting in about fifteen minutes. Why don't you call me later this evening and we can have that talk then."

"Okay, no problem. I'll call you later and I hope whatever is going on turns it's self around for you soon. I don't like to see you this down," he said, exiting her office.

When he reached the elevator, he knew he'd just missed his opportunity to talk to her. He knew talking about it at her job wasn't a good choice so he'll put it off until later. They needed to talk about calling off the wedding. She was already down about something and he didn't want to add more bad information on top of whatever else she was going through. He would let Cecily know that he would talk to Victoria and fix things. Today just wasn't a good day. Hopefully by the time he finally got up the nerve to have the conversation he knew they needed to have that Victoria's day would be better.

~~

Back in the office, Tyrone briefed Duron and Mike on his trip to Boston. All three of them had been busy working on separate projects with their teams and did not have a chance to talk in the week that Tyrone had been back from Boston. Mike was patched in via conference call since he was back in California with his wife.

He was glad that they both agreed with him that the business deal with Turner and his partners would be a good move and they decided to definitely agree to work on the project. Tyrone informed them that he needed to make one more trip to Boston to iron out the final details once they agreed on them. He already began working out the necessary re-designs according to Turner's specifications and his assistant was making those changes for him. He would need to make another trip to Boston to go over all of the changes. He also needed to take a quick trip to Washington to tour the winery, vineyards and office space in order to get a better feel for what needed to be done.

On a personal level, he wasn't happy about making another trip to Boston. He couldn't imagine going all that way and not seeing Victoria, but that's exactly what he would do. He missed her more than he thought he would in the week since his return. She had called several times leaving messages making sure he was okay and again apologizing for the mess she'd caused. She also ended each message telling him that she loved him. He didn't call her back because she hadn't once said the words that he wanted to hear. He wanted to hear her say that she had broken things off with Turner and had come to her senses. He had been tempted to call her back, but he couldn't keep putting himself back in that situation with her. No matter how much he loved her he couldn't do that to himself. It wasn't that she wasn't worth it because she was. It was too painful for them both.

After the meeting, Duron stuck around to talk.

"Tyrone, I don't want to pry, but clearly something is going on with you. I admit you did a great job on the Warfield project with Turner, but something else is going on and you seem a bit distracted. You know I'm here if you need to talk bro," Duron said.

"I know and I appreciate it. It's something I need to work through on a personal level. For now I'm trying to put it on the back burner so that it doesn't impact work. We are very busy right now and there isn't room for distractions. Before you go, can I ask you a question?" he said.

"Anything, bro, you know that," Duron said.

"I know that before you and Taija got married, you had some problems. I know for a while things were pretty rough and no one thought that you two would get back together. What did you do to pull things back together with Taija? Was it the strength of your love for one another? Is love really powerful enough to overcome any issue?" he inquired.

"Are the problems you're having about a woman?" Duron asked, shocked.

"You said I could ask anything. Can I ask and you just answer without you asking a bunch of questions I don't have an answer to right now?"

Duron didn't press. Very seldom did Tyrone discuss his private life so he followed his lead.

"Okay, let me see if I can come up with the best and most honest way to respond to that. How did I pull things together? For starters I was stubborn. When Taija tried to explain things to me that would have fixed our situation a lot sooner, I was too pig-headed to listen. My sister actually helped me realize I was being a fool and that's when I knew that no matter what I had to do, I was going to get her back. I wasn't going to stop until she was mine again. Luckily she was forgiving and I didn't have to beg to hard," Duron laughed at the memory.

"I remember Mike telling me what happened at the hospital benefit," Tyrone said.

"I had no doubt that she was the woman for me and I would do anything to make sure she knew that and that she knew I would always be hers. I would have done anything to get her back. I poured my heart out to her, not worrying about being all manly. I would have crawled to her if I thought that's what it would take. Again, no crawling was needed and our love was strong enough that nothing was going to keep us apart. Real, true love is like that. Once it hits you, nothing, and I mean nothing, can keep two people apart who are meant to be together. That's how it was for Taija and I."

Duron waited to see if Tyrone would divulge any more information without him having to pry. If he was asking about love, whatever was going on with him was big. That was a word that he never thought he'd hear come out of Tyrone's mouth.

"You and Taija have a love that is to be admired. Not everyone has that. It seems love is pretty tricky. It's not as easy to do and have it work out for you as it is to just say the word," Tyrone declared.

"I'm trying not to ask questions like you asked me to, but you know you have me wondering what's going on here. You know you can tell me anything if it will help get it off of your chest. You are struggling with something and I can see how much it's bothering you. I know something is going on with you and a woman and since I know you never get too involved with them, this one must be very special. Are you in love with someone?"

Tyrone hesitated, but decided to admit it to his best friend. It was time he told someone.

"Yeah D, I am in love with someone and before you ask any more questions, let's leave it at that for now."

"Okay, I can do that. I know admitting that you are in love with someone is hard for you. Again, you know where to reach me any time of the day or night when you need to."

"Thanks bro, I appreciate that. I won't hold you any longer since I know your wife is expecting you for her appointment, so don't be late," Tyrone said, feeling a little better after talking to Duron.

"You're right about that. Taija is crazy when it comes to me making all of her doctor appointments. I'll check on you later."

"Cool. Also, I ordered a special gift for the twins that arrived while I was in Boston. I'll bring it by the house tomorrow evening," Tyrone said.

"Already spoiling my kids and they aren't even here yet. Taija and I are going to be in trouble," Duron joked.

"Yeah, yeah," he responded, knowing Duron was right.

He hoped Duron's words rang true for him when it came to love as well. If he and Victoria were really in love, he was expecting things to work out. If not, it wasn't really meant to be. That's not something he was willing to believe, but the ball wasn't in his court. Victoria was the decision maker. She held all the cards.

~~

Tyrone drove up to Duron's house to drop off the gift he'd ordered for his soon to be born godchildren. Duron was spending more time working at home to be closer to Taija, especially in the evenings when he would normally stay late at the office. Carrying twins, she was having a hard time doing normal things for herself around the house and he knew that Duron didn't feel comfortable leaving her alone for long stretches of time. His mother came out to the house often to help and Taija's mother had also flown in a few times, but Tyrone knew that Duron only felt comfortable if he was home tending to her.

Duron was standing at the door when Tyrone pulled up

after begin buzzed in at the gate to the community.

"What's up man?" Tyrone asked walking into the house after removing an extra-large box from the back of his truck.

"Nothing, just catching up on some paperwork."

"It's been a busy day at the office. I'm going to put the box in the nursery. Don't let Taija open it until the babies get here," he said going up the stairs.

"I'll try, but you know how stubborn she is. What she wants she gets and if she wants in that box, I'm not going to stop her," he joked.

"Where's Taija?" Tyrone asked.

"She's on the lower level waiting for something to come on the television. Something about an announcement for Victoria's engagement or something like that."

Tyrone's antenna went up at the mention of Victoria's name.

"Okay, let me put this down and I'll go down to say hi," he said.

He placed the box in the closet in the twin's room, hopefully out of Taija's sight until he was ready for her to see what was inside. After doing so, he headed down to the lower level to see her. She looked up just as he'd hit the last step.

"Tyrone, it's good to see you," she said when he joined her in the theater room.

"You look beautiful as usual," he said. "Duron said you were planted in front of the television. What are you so engrossed in?" he asked.

"My friend Victoria, you remember her right?"

Boy did he ever. He did nothing daily but remember her. He wished it were different, but no such luck.

"Yeah, I remember her."

"There is a big story about her engagement on the television. I missed it due to all the sleep these babies make me take part in every day. Victoria sent me a text that it's coming back on again in a few minutes and I don't want to miss it this time."

"Is that so," Tyrone said just as a picture of Victoria and Turner appeared on the screen. He couldn't help but watch it even though he didn't want to.

The show did the official announcement of the engagement and pending marriage of the two. It was big news because of the high profile nature of Turner's family. A brief history was done on Turner's family and the winery and vineyards and then more information was told of how Turner finally proposed to the childhood friend he had always been in love with. Tyrone doubted that.

"I'm so excited for her," Tyrone heard Taija say. "Doesn't she look beautiful?"

"She sure does," he said reluctantly, not that he didn't believe that she was beautiful. It was because he didn't want to see her standing in the arms of Turner on national television.

He'd seen enough as he leaned over to kiss Taija on the cheek.

"I'm heading out. There is a box in the nursery that you are not to open until after the babies get here," he said.

"What? Why did you tell me? Now I'm going to want to know what it is," she said disappointed. She loved all of the gifts that people were giving them. Her excitement about the pending arrival of the babies went to a new level every time she received another gift for them.

"I wasn't going to tell you, but I don't want you coming

down on Duron about the box in case you saw it in the closet in their room so no peeking," he said.

"Alright and only because it's you will I oblige. You are already spoiling them and they aren't even here yet," she said.

"That's what your husband said and I'm not listening to either one of you," he said making his exit.

"Oh, and the next time you talk to Victoria, tell her I said congratulations and I hope she's very happy," he said, not meaning any of what he'd just said.

"I will," Taija said turning back to the news.

Tyrone went up the steps and headed for the front door, not even stopping to tell Duron he was leaving.

"Whoa, where's the fire," Duron said, seeing Tyrone's fast pace for the door.

Tyrone stopped in his tracks.

"Before you leave, Mike is on the line for you real quick. He called and I told him you were still here," Duron said handing the phone to Tyrone.

"What do you want Mike," Tyrone said angrily.

Tyrone couldn't pull back the anger before it laced his words to Mike.

"Did I piss you off or something man?" Mike asked, not sure where the anger in Tyrone's voice was coming from.

"No, I'm sorry about that. What's up?" he asked calmer.

He listened and Mike gave his input on the latest contracts that he and Duron had both looked over.

"Loren says to ask Taija did she see the story on Victoria and Turner on the news," Mike said.

"Tell her Taija was just watching it," he replied.

He heard Mike tell her before returning to the phone.

"Hey Ty, did you happen to see Victoria when you were

in Boston?" Mike asked.

"Save it Mike," Tyrone replied with anger in his voice.

"Whoa, bro. What's gotten under your skin?" Duron asked, being able to not only hear, but see Tyrone's anger.

Tyrone knew he was being aggressive with his response. He pulled it back.

"Nothing."

Tyrone handed the phone back to Duron then looked away, clearly dismissing any more conversation.

"Mike, listen, that's it on our end. I'll touch base with you later. Kiss my sister for me," Duron said, ending the call and then turning his attention to Tyrone.

"Ty, you wanna tell me what's eating at you? I know we talked yesterday and clearly whatever was going on then, is still going on now. What gives and don't even try telling me it's nothing. I hear you tear Mike's head off for no reason so spill it. I'm not going to let up until you do."

Tyrone said nothing at first. He knew he needed to tell someone so that he could get it off of his chest. There was a time he could tell Mike and Duron everything that was going on with him. This was no different so he decided to confide in his friend.

He turned so that he was facing Duron head on.

"It's Victoria, D," he said, feeling relief at finally being able to say her name out loud to someone.

"Victoria? Taija's Victoria? What about her?" Duron said before realization set in for him.

"Guess man," Tyrone said, not sure he would be able to actually say the words.

"Wait, let's back up to the recent conversation where Mike asked you about seeing Victoria in Texas. You said nothing happened, but clearly it did. Then there is the conversation we had yesterday. This all ties back to Victoria?" he asked.

"Yeah, it does," Tyrone admitted. "Boy does it ever."

He hesitated before continuing on, not sure how much to share.

"I can see this is going to be deep," Duron said.

"She put it on me D, like you wouldn't believe."

"Maybe you need to start all the way from the beginning. Let's go in the kitchen and get a beer. This sounds like a beer kind of conversation."

Once they had their beers and were seated at the counter, Tyrone decided it was best to start from the beginning. He needed to get the whole story out.

"What about Taija?"

"Don't worry about her. She's probably asleep by now. The strange thing is, she is most comfortable in the recliners down there than in the bed upstairs so she naps down there frequently. A few nights ago, she made me sleep down there because she was more comfortable than she knew that she would be in the bed. It worked for her, but did a killing on me. My legs are too long for that," he said and laughed.

"I bet that was uncomfortable for you."

"Yeah, but we compromised. During the day, she gets to sleep and nap down there, but at night, it's the bedroom. So now, talk. What's going on?" Duron asked.

"Okay, I'm sure you know that when I was in Texas for that conference that I ran into Victoria. Once I realized it was her, we talked a bit and agreed to share dinner after the conference was over. That dinner led to a night of the best sex of my entire life and you know that's saying something."

Duron knew he was right. The only person who had surpassed him when it came to the women department was Tyrone.

"Okay, so you had sex. What's that got to do with the bad mood you're in?" Duron asked.

"We've been sort of seeing each other since then. Not right away, but a few times since then."

"Ty, the woman is engaged to be married, man. First, why would you even sleep with a woman who is engaged to another man when you were in Texas? Then why would you continue doing so? That's not how we operate man. You know the code."

Tyrone knew what he was talking about. They never, ever ventured into another man's territory unless it was clear that things weren't serious between said man and said woman. In this case, the engagement was considered serious.

"I know D, but I didn't know she was engaged when we slept together in Texas. She was not wearing that gigantic ring at the time; I would have noticed that. If nothing else, she should have said something around the time when clothes started flying all over the place. All bets were off once she was naked though. No man would be able to resist that body," he said.

"Okay, I'll give you that because you didn't know. Have you slept with her since finding out? Like after the baby shower?"

Duron remember something from the night of the shower. He saw Victoria when she came up from the lower level. Duron thought at the time that she looked a little disheveled. He then remembered seeing Tyrone come up a few minutes after her looking like a man who had just won the lottery, all happy and sexually relaxed.

He looked at Tyrone with shock on his face.

"Ty, tell me you did not do that woman in my house," he demanded, while also smiling at how slick his friend was.

"Okay, I won't tell you, but yeah I did. I'm telling you D, I cannot resist that woman. Well that is until recently."

"What happened recently? I'm assuming you saw her while you were in Boston," Duron said.

"It wasn't planned, but yeah I did. We had agreed to stay away from each other. What we didn't do was decide to not talk to each other. We would talk just about every night and the phone sex was just as good as the real thing."

"Too much information Ty, really, too much. Just stick to the basics, with a little less graphics."

"Right," Tyrone said, with a devious smile on his face.

"This is better than those steamy romance novels Taija reads," Duron said, waiting for Tyrone to continue.

"I talked to her while I was there and one thing led to another which led to me getting sexed like never before at her house. It was after that, that things turned ugly."

"How?" Duron inquired.

"She said she was in love with me. I'm also in love with her and I told her so. I asked her about her engagement to Turner and if she was going to break it off and she said no, even though she admitted to not being in love with him, or get this, she also admitted that they have never slept together. This is a guy she is going to marry D."

Tyrone noticed Duron was about to ask another question, but he continued on first.

"Wait, that's not the half of it. I also spotted Turner lip locking with a beauty the morning I left to come back to Atlanta. There is something not right about whatever is going on with Victoria and Turner, but she won't tell me what's going on. She's willing to sleep with me, but she's not willing to end whatever they have so that she and I could have an honest try at a relationship."

"Whoa. You said relationship, bro. That's a mighty big word for you. I've never heard you use that word in the same sentence as a woman's name. You really are serious about her. Wait 'til Taija hears about this."

Tyrone turned very serious.

"No, D, you can't tell Taija. Whatever you do, do not tell her anything about this."

"Oh I won't if you are that adamant about it, but I'm sure sooner or later, Victoria is going to tell Taija about all of this. How did you and Victoria end things?"

"I ended it when I got dressed and left after I realized I was being a fool. You know my thoughts on women and love. I saw myself going down a path that wasn't leading to anything good other than some more incredible sex," he said, looking at Duron realizing he once again was giving away too much information.

He stopped Duron before he could mention that again.

"I know D, too much information. I love her and she is an incredible woman. It's not just about the sex. You know I can get that just about anywhere. It's her I want. At least I thought I did until I realized she doesn't want the same thing. Maybe she does and doesn't know how to get out of this engagement with Turner. Either way, she wasn't willing to talk about it with me and I asked her if she would break it off and she said no. That was my cue to leave so I did. On top of that, my mother has been to see my grandmother and she wants to see me. Can you believe that? She's been gone most of my life and she pops up wanting to get to know me and start over."

"Wow man. Now I see why you've been in a crappy mood lately," Duron replied.

"Yeah, sorry about that. Between this mess with Victoria and my mother whom I can honestly say I hate, my week has been steadily been going down-hill."

Duron sympathized with his friend. He remembered the many nights in the dorm at college when Tyrone would talk about his home life and how much his mother's betrayal had hurt him. He has never been able to forgive her and sometimes when Tyrone got in a mood similar to the one he's in now, nothing could seem to pull him out of it other than the passing of time.

"Ty, don't let this consume you. Don't let this harden your heart when it comes to women. I never thought I'd ever hear you say you were in love with a woman and I'm glad to hear that it has finally happened for you, even under these circumstances. Maybe Victoria isn't the one for you. At least you know that you are capable of opening up your heart to loving a woman. I know you still have hurt and pain when it comes to your mother and I can't tell you what to do. All I can say is I love you like a brother. Hell, you, Mike and I are closer than I am with my brothers. I want nothing but good things for you. Don't close yourself off completely from the love of a woman or the love of your mother. Just think about it. I know she's been gone for a long time, but she's still the woman that gave birth to you. Maybe one day you'll be able to at least sit down to have a conversation with her. Just think about what I'm saying. Now as far as this mess with Victoria is concerned, walk away. I know you want her and I know you love her, but for now, walk away. It's clear to me that she has a lot to work through and she can't do that if she's feeling pressured, so walk away. If things are meant to be, they will work out. Don't let this upset or distract you. When I told you I would do anything back when Taija and I were having problems, that would not have been the case if another man was in the picture. In those situations, that woman needs to figure out what she wants to do. Pressuring her could only lead to more indecisiveness because she would only be thinking with her heart and she needs her heart and her mind in this one for it to work out. I say give her time to do that. If it takes too long, then let it go. You saw the announcement today. I saw it when it first came out. Clearly she's made up her mind to marry this guy so don't take yourself through this. There is only so much you can control and this isn't it. You can't make her leave Turner and chose you. I know you wouldn't want that if she were pressured into it. You want her to do it willingly because there is no doubt that you are who she wants to be with. Let her get to that point."

"You're right D and I know it. I've just let it get me down, but talking to you has made me feel much better," he said, smiling, letting his friend know that he was fine.

"Look, let's go out back and shoot a few hoops."

"That sounds like a good idea," Tyrone said.

"Let me go check on Taija and I'll meet you out back. You know where the balls are. The night lights should already be on.

Tyrone already felt much better as he headed towards Duron's outside basketball court. Even as night began to fall, it was lit up like the middle of the day with the surrounding lights. The best decision he'd made in a long time was to come clean with his best friend. He'd been carrying the burden of the hurt from his mother and from Victoria around and it was impacting his relationship with Duron and Mike. He also knew his work was suffering because he was unable to concentrate.

"Alright bro, let's take some of your frustrations out on the court and leave it out of the office. Make sure you call Mike and apologize for being short with him on the phone. Unless you've told him what you told me I'm sure he's wondering what he did to piss you off. You don't have to tell him everything, but tell him something."

Tyrone had already been thinking about doing that once he got home. He knew he owed Mike and apology and an explanation.

"I hear you D and I'll take care of that tonight. For now, let's get this game on so I can show you what it feels like to get beat on your own court."

Chapter 14

"Dinner was really good baby," Taija said to Duron as he proceeded to clean away the dishes from the table.

"I'm glad you enjoyed it," he said leaning over to plant a kiss on her lips before heading into the kitchen.

Taija could hear the phone ringing in the other room.

"Taija, Victoria's on the phone," Duron said handing the cordless phone to her so that she wouldn't have to get up. He knew that carrying twins was getting more and more complicated for his wife when it came to her moving around.

"Victoria, hey girl. I'm so happy to hear from you," Taija said. "I saw the announcement on the television last night and I can't wait to hear all the plans you're making for the ceremony."

Her cheerful sound turned to one of worry when all she heard in response was crying.

"Victoria, what's wrong?" she said. Her question was again met with more crying, even louder now.

"You have to stop crying and tell me what's wrong," she

said into the phone.

"Is everything okay," Duron asked when he entered the room and saw the look of concern on his wife's face. He had no doubt Victoria was about to share with her what had been going on with her and Tyrone. He didn't want her to know that he knew what was going on.

"Yes, Victoria is just upset about something. Everything is good. Let me talk to her and find out what's going on."

"Okay, I'm going to let you two talk. I'll go and straighten up downstairs. Holler when you're ready to go up to bed," he said before leaving her to console her friend. If Victoria was in any state similar to the one Tyrone had been in, Taija was in for a long night of girl talk.

Taija waited until Victoria's cries had subsided before she spoke again.

"Victoria, I can't help you if you don't tell me what's wrong. Why are you crying?" she asked.

"I'm sorry Tai. I thought I would be able to keep it together, but when I heard your voice, all I could do was cry. I'm so screwed up right now. I couldn't think of anyone I wanted to tell my problems to but you. I hope that's okay."

"Yes it's okay as long as you get around to telling them to me. So far all I've heard are sobs from you. What's wrong," she asked again.

"My life is falling apart Tai and I don't know how I've gotten myself into this or how to get out of it," she said with pain and sorrow in her voice.

"Victoria, start from the beginning."

"Okay."

For the next hour, Victoria shared with Taija all that she had been going through including her fake engagement to

Turner and the start of her affair with Tyrone.

Taija was stunned. She didn't know her friend was going through so much. She suspected something wasn't right about Victoria's engagement to Turner. Taija knew them both pretty well during her time in Boston and she knew that they were life-long friends. She never suspected that they were ever anything more than friends and she didn't think that in the time since she'd left that they'd suddenly found out that they were in love and wanted to get married.

She remembered watching their interaction at her baby shower and what she didn't see was love. She saw the same old friendship that she had seen when she lived in Boston. No matter what, she was going to support her friend. If she said she was getting married, Taija knew she wouldn't question it. She would be right by her side supporting her as Victoria had done for her. That's what friends did.

"Victoria, why didn't you tell Tyrone the truth and save yourself and him all of this misery. I know he would understand. What I don't understand is how can you go ahead with a marriage knowing it's only a temporary one and in the mean time you could lose the love of the man you say makes you feel complete? Do you know how often that comes around for any woman? Very rarely and you are willing to walk away from it for the sake of friendship? If I were you, I would question my friendship with Turner if he would allow you to give up on true love with Tyrone so that he can gain his fortune."

"Tai, Turner doesn't know about Tyrone. I didn't tell him," she admitted.

"Victoria, no. Stop this! Everyone needs to come clean here. Look at all the hurt and misery this fake marriage is going to cause. You love Tyrone. I hear it in your voice. If I were in your presence, I know I'd be able to see it on your face as well. Don't give up that kind of happiness so that someone else could get what they want. Turner needs to find another way to do this that doesn't include you giving up a year of your life and the man of your dreams," she pleaded.

"What do I do Taija? I don't even know where to start."

"For starters, do you love Tyrone enough to sacrifice your friendship with Turner and have the happiness you have been seeking your entire life?"

"Yes," Victoria said without hesitating. "When Tyrone left here I have been completely miserable. I miss him so much and I need him. I don't want to do this with Turner anymore and I've made a complete mess of my life."

"It's not something you can't fix. For starters, I think you need to start with talking to Turner. Something tells me that if you are honest with him, he would understand and would not want you to sacrifice so much for him. The two of you have been friends for many years and you made this deal thinking it would be okay because you weren't involved with anyone. Now that you are and you're in love, I think this negates any agreement the two of you have made. Just talk to him. After you do, reach out to Tyrone and come clean with him. You said he already suspects things were not on the up and up with the engagement. He also knows that it's not an intimate relationship between you and Turner, so I think he'll be happy to hear that you've chosen to be with him."

"You're right. I'm going to call Turner tomorrow and tell him we need to talk. I've been crying all evening since I got home and I don't feel like talking to anyone else tonight. You've made me feel so much better. I knew talking to you would help, Tai. Thank you for being my friend and for helping me see clearly what I need to do."

"I'm always here any time you need me."

"How are my godchildren doing?"

"As soon as you said that, one or both of them kicked me," Taija said, rubbing her belly to calm the babies. "They're doing fine. Not too much longer and you'll be able to hold and spoil them as I'm sure you are looking forward to doing."

"Yes I am," Victoria replied happily, no longer sad and crying.

"Call me and let me know how things turn out. If I need to smack Tyrone around a little bit to help bring him to his senses, just let me know. I'd be more than happy to do that."

"I sure will. Thank Duron for letting me take up all of your time tonight. I'll talk to you in a few days."

Victoria felt like a weight had been lifted just by talking to her friend. She knew all along what she needed to do. She just needed to talk to someone and spill all of the things that had been weighing her down.

She was sure of a few things now and the first of those was that she wasn't going to marry Turner and she was in love with Tyrone and had no plans to allow him to just walk away feeling hurt because she had chosen Turner over him. She first needed to talk to Turner and then she would reach out to Tyrone, hopeful that he was still willing to talk to her.

~~

Duron came into the room just as Taija was finished with her call with Victoria.

"You knew didn't you?" she asked her husband.

"What," he said, innocently.

"Don't try me Duron. It's not nice to fool with a pregnant woman, especially one carrying not one, but two of your babies at once," she said.

"Yeah I knew. Tyrone confided in me a few days ago when he stopped by. It was the day you were watching the televised announcement of her engagement and he saw it."

Before Taija could tear his head off for keeping it from her, he added, "but we're going to let them work it out or not work it out. Whatever it is, we're going to support them. Tyrone is my friend just as Victoria is yours. As much as we'd like to see them together, this working or not working out is not up to us," he said walking up behind her as she sat in the chair and began massaging her shoulders.

Taija slumped her shoulders when she realized Duron was right.

"I know. I just want to see them both happy and they are miserable apart, wouldn't you agree?" she asked, closing her eyes, enjoying the feel of stress leaving her body with every stroke of his hands across her tense shoulders.

"My concern is making sure that you're happy, baby. Tyrone and Victoria can work out their own troubles. Right now I want to know what else I can do to make you happy. Ready for a foot rub?" he asked.

"I'm ready for something," Taija said, purring from his touch. When his hand slid down from her shoulder, into her blouse to cup her very swollen breasts and sensitive nipples, she felt like a lump of aroused clay.

"I'm ready too," Duron said, leaning down to place soft kisses across the back of Taija's neck while continuing to excite her more and more with his caresses.

"I bet you are, Mr. Ever-ready. Why don't you come around in front of me and show me just how ready you are."

"Not a good idea baby. I know I shouldn't have started this. The doctor said no sex until after the babies were born. You are already having some problems and sex could cause you to go into early labor and we don't want that," he said, trying to sound convincing.

"I know, but that doesn't mean we can't do other things." She loved how things never got old or dull between the two of them.

Duron came around to face Taija and before he could bend over to plant a kiss on her lips, she reached for the zipper of his jeans that was clearly having a hard time containing his straining erection.

"Like I said, we could do other things. How about I lick you first and then it'll be your turn," she said with great excitement.

Duron liked how his wife thought as he closed his eyes and let her have her way with him until it was his turn to do the same for her.

~~

Tyrone was feeling a little better as he walked toward his office. Even Duron had commented that Tyrone seemed to be in a better mood than he had been a few days ago. Tyrone realized it wasn't fair for him to take his frustrations out on everyone else. He even received a call from one of his no-strings attached friends and they were planning to do dinner and a movie soon at his condo. It was time he got back in the swing of things. Tyrone knew he needed to move on from Victoria and the best way to do that was to turn his attention away from her and back to other women. He hadn't heard from her lately and as much as he wanted to talk to her, he refrained from calling her. He realized that since the televised announcement of her engagement to Turner, several more live television interviews of them were broadcasted on several channels and there were a couple of write-ups in national newspapers. He wasn't sure when those had been done, but it was a sure sign to him that things were pretty much over between he and Victoria.

Things were going to finally be looking up for him as long as he continued concentrating on forgetting about Victoria. It was time he moved on. He vowed to smile through the rest of his day. That at least was his plan until he walked back to his office and his secretary told him he had a visitor waiting. She told him it was his mother and the world around him crashed and burned.

He looked at his secretary in a manner that visibly scared her. He then softened his features because it wasn't her fault. There was no way his secretary would know that the woman sitting in his office may have given birth to him, but she wasn't his mother. He gathered every bit of strength he had and went into his office.

He didn't say a word as he entered and she stood. He looked at her briefly before going around her and settling in behind his desk without any type of greeting.

"I guess I expected that," she said when he sat down without saying a word to her.

"Why are you here," he said gruffly, making sure she knew he wasn't happy to see her.

"I spoke to your grandmother and she said you didn't want to see me, but I still wanted to see you, so I flew in today. I was hoping we could talk a little Tyrone."

The sound of his name coming from her turned his stomach.

"How'd you find me?" he asked.

"You're aren't hard to find. I saw that wonderful article about you and this company in Black Enterprise magazine. I only had to look up the company when I got to town. I figured if I called first, you wouldn't want to see me."

"I still don't," he said without pause. "You've seen me so you can leave now," he said, dismissing her by pretending to look over some papers left on his desk.

"Tyrone could we please just talk? I think I need to explain everything to you. If I did, I think you'd understand I wasn't well back then. I wasn't in a place to take care of you," she said. "I knew you would be better off with my parents."

"I can't do this with you right now," he said angrily. "In fact, I can't do this with you ever. I don't want to see you. I don't want you here, so get out and never come back!" he shouted.

As if she hadn't heard him, she continued on trying to explain her leaving him all those years ago and he didn't want to hear it. Before he knew what was happening, he was up out of his chair, leaning over his desk screaming at her to get out. He must have been extremely loud because he looked up and saw Duron followed by his secretary enter his office to see what the problem was.

"Tyrone, what's going on?" Duron asked with concern at the scene before him. He had never seen Tyrone yelling at a woman before.

Tyrone didn't respond. He continued staring at the woman with more hatred than Duron had ever known Tyrone to display. He saw the woman that Tyrone had been screaming at and inquired.

"Ma'am, can I help you with something? What's going on here?"

"My name is JoAnn Davis and I'm Tyrone's mother," she said.

"No she isn't," Tyrone shouted out. "Giving birth to me doesn't make you my mother and I want you out of my office right now," he shouted again at the top of his voice.

He was clearly more agitated than Duron had ever seen him and the only way to calm him was going to be to escort the woman out.

"Ma'am, I'm sorry. If Tyrone says he doesn't want you hear, I'm going to have to ask you to leave, please," Duron said, trying to escort her slowly towards the door.

She walked with Duron, but turned to Tyrone one last time before leaving.

"I'm sorry because I didn't mean to upset you. I only wanted to talk to you," she said on a whisper as she gave one last glance in his direction before leaving with her shoulders slumped in surrender.

When she was gone, Duron came back into Tyrone's office and closed the door behind him.

"Ty, are you alright? I gave instructions that she is to never be allowed in the office again. Her name will be listed with security downstairs."

Duron tried to calm Tyrone down as he watched him pace back and forth.

"Why would she come here knowing I wouldn't want to see her, D?"

"I don't know, but she's not here anymore so sit and calm down."

"I can't calm down. How dare she come here as if she

expected me to be okay with her?"

"Ty, I know this is bad, but calm down."

Duron instructed Tyrone's secretary to get him a bottle of water.

When she returned with the water, Tyrone drank it down without pausing. He then finally stopped pacing and sat back down behind his desk.

"Now that you're cool again, tell me what happened besides her just showing up. What did she say?" Duron asked.

"I don't know anything she said. I couldn't get beyond the fact that she was in my office as if we could actually work things out because she showed up today. I'm good now. Thanks, D."

"Tyrone, you really need to talk this out with someone. This has been eating away at you for years. It's probably time you dealt with this. Even though she's not allowed here anymore, I don't think that will be the last you'll see of her."

"I know you're right, but for now, I can't deal with anything. I think I'm going to head out for the day. I'm going to work from home the rest of the day," he said, standing to grab files he would need to take with him.

"Ty, take the day off and do anything but work today. You need to relax and you know you won't be able to concentrate on work and I need you in tip top shape when it comes to the projects. We have some pretty heavy hitters and we can't afford to miss a step with personal issues."

"Thanks D for having my back. You know I appreciate you bro," he said walking out with him towards the elevator. "I'll probably do some work on my car. "

"Okay, cool. I know that calms you so do that. I'll check

on you later," he said as he watched his friend, who had seemed to relax over the past few days had once again reached a boiling point. He also realized Tyrone needed someone other than him to talk to. If he thought it would help, he would call Tyrone's grandmother, but that's not what he needed right now. What he needed was a face to face conversation with another person who loved him like a son.

Duron reached for his cell and called his own mother for help.

Chapter 15

Victoria waited all day for Turner to return her phone call. She'd left him several messages that they needed to talk. She was hoping that they would be able to talk before the end of the week so that they could get beyond all this. She knew that at first he would be hurt, but they needed to stop the train wreck that was occurring in her life. As much as she cherished their friendship, what they were planning to do wouldn't benefit either of them, especially him, though he thought it would because of what he would be getting in the end.

She was about to try his number again when her doorbell rang. She checked and saw Turner standing on the other side of her door and she opened it quickly.

"I've been trying to reach you all day," she said as he entered.

"I know. I've been contemplating a conversation that we need to have for a while now and I wasn't sure how to handle it and until I did, I waited to reach back out to you," he said, sounding sullen.

"Turner, what's wrong? Has something happened?" she asked, concerned.

He was about to speak when his cell phone rang. He apologized and answered it.

At the end of his call, he told her he had to leave because he had an emergency. He knew that they really needed to talk and he would give her a call so that they could. He told her he didn't want to have a quick chit chat, but that they really needed to talk.

She agreed, but wanted to let him go handle whatever the emergency situation was.

"I'm sorry. I know we really needed to talk. Why don't we have dinner tomorrow night?" he suggested.

"That's sounds like a great idea. I hope things work out okay with your emergency," she said.

"It will," he said, giving her a kiss on the cheek before heading back out.

All Victoria could think about was the fact that they'd just missed an opportunity to clear the air and straighten things out so that they could figure out how to move forward and still maintain their friendship.

She had no other plans for the evening because her plan was to leave her evening open so that she and Turner could work things out. Now she was left with a free evening to once again obsess over not hearing from Tyrone.

Now with time on her hands, Victoria was upset. She really didn't plan for things to go on so long now that she'd decided to not marry Turner. It appears the conversation between them would have to wait a little longer. The emergency that he had spoken to her about was now going to postpone their conversation for another day or so.

She had hoped to be done with this by now and be in the

midst of working things out with Tyrone. She had to wait an additional day. She could do that. Once this was dealt with, she could move on with her life, hopefully one that included Tyrone.

She missed him so much. She had not heard from him since he'd left her house when he was last in Boston. She guessed another day wouldn't hurt before reaching out to Tyrone to confess everything and hoped that he would forgive her.

~~

Tyrone entered the supper club and looked around for Duron. They were meeting for drinks and some pool. He knew that Duron was trying everything to take Tyrone's mind off of his troubles of late. After leaving the office, Duron called inviting him out. A few of Taija's sorority sisters had stopped over to keep Taija company for a few hours so he thought it was a good time to go out.

Tyrone spotted Duron, already engaged in a game with the owner and one of their good friends, Jason.

"Ty," Jason greeted him as he joined them.

"What's up man," he replied. "Hey D. What's up with this crowd in the middle of the week? Business never slows down here, huh?" Tyrone inquired, looking around at the packed house. He knew Jason, whom they all referred to as Jase, ran the best supper club in Atlanta.

"Never. If it did, I'd have to come to you to get a loan to make ends meet, so I welcome the crowd every night," Jase responded.

"So do I," Tyrone laughed.

"I guess you're here to beat this fool in some pool," Jase said to Tyrone while pointing at Duron.

"Hey, this fool is planning to take everybody's money

tonight, starting with you," Duron replied.

"Luckily I have the evening off and can show you how a real champ shoots pool," Jase challenged.

Duron was about to check with Tyrone with how things were going since they'd last spoke earlier in the day when he looked up to see his brother Brian enter. Brian hardly ever ventured into downtown Atlanta. Duron waved him over.

"Hey bro, what brings you in tonight?" he asked.

After greeting Tyrone and Jase, Brian asked to speak to Duron in private.

"Sure. Ty, go easy on Jason in my absence," he said walking away with his brother.

"What's up Brian?" Duron said as they sat at the bar.

"I have a problem and I'm trying to figure out how to handle it. I ran into a friend of mine over the weekend at the wedding of one of my students."

Brian was a college professor.

"This friend mentioned that he was now living in Baltimore and recently ran into Sherry. You remember Sherry Braxton I use to be involved with?"

"Yeah, I remember her," Duron said.

"Well he said she had a child that looked to be about two years old and that he assumed the little girl was mine because she looked exactly like Loren. He said the little girl looked more like me than Sherry. When he mentioned that, he said Sherry got nervous and said that he was mistaken, that the little girl wasn't mine, but that the father was someone else. D, he was sure that the little girl looked so much like Loren that anyone who saw her would think that Loren had a long lost little girl living in Baltimore."

"What are you saying Brian, that this little girl is your

daughter?"

"I don't know Duron. If this little girl is in fact about two years old, then yes, it's possible Sherry may be living in Baltimore with my daughter."

"Wow. What do you want to do?"

"I'm planning to go to Baltimore to confront her. I know where her parents live and I thought I'd start with them to try and reach her."

"I don't think that's a good idea Brian. If she wanted you to know where she was, especially if she has your daughter, she would have told you."

"I know, but it's been bothering me since the wedding. I know my relationship ended with her on very bad terms, but if that's my daughter, I need to know," Brian said.

"You're right, but I don't think that you should just pop up on her in Baltimore without even seeing the little girl for yourself first. Let me have a friend of mine who's a private eye help with this. He should be able to do some checking and get you a picture and then you can see if there is a resemblance. If so, then I'd say pay Sherry a visit and demand to have a blood test to see if in fact you are the father."

Brian thought on the idea for a moment and realized Duron was right.

"Have him call me and I'll give him the information on Sherry that I have, starting with where her parents live and let's see what he can come up with."

"I'll call him tomorrow. Why don't you join us for a game of pool since you're already here," Duron said.

"No thanks. I have a ton of papers to grade. Taija told me you were here when I called the house so I just came down to talk to you. I have a lot of work to do so I'm going to head back home. Thanks for the help," Brian said.

"I'll reach out to my friend and have him give you a call tomorrow. Keep me posted on how things turn out. No sudden trips to Baltimore. You have no idea what you'd be walking in on if you did."

"I hear you bro. I'll wait to see what the private eye comes up with."

When Duron rejoined the pool game, Tyrone was alone.

"Where's Jase?" he asked.

"He had to take care of something and said he'd be back."

"I got the most interesting call today," Tyrone said knowing Duron knew who he was talking about.

"Did you? From who?" he asked, knowing the answer.

"Your mom called and invited me over. She said she hadn't seen me in a while and wanted to check up on me. Even though I told her I was fine, she said she wanted to see for herself and told me to stop over Saturday at noon and hung up before I could even say whether I could or could not come by. I guess that means I don't have a choice. Any idea what she really wants?" he asked.

"Not a clue man. I guess you better show up and find out. You know my mom, don't let her have to come looking for you."

"I know and I'm going. I'm just saying, you could have given a brother a heads up that you were calling out the troops for support. You know I appreciate you sharing your mom with me. Just don't blind side me with surprise requests from her unless it includes something that she baked," he said laughing.

It felt good to laugh. Tyrone had almost forgotten what that was like because a lot had been going on in his life lately.

He was missing Victoria like crazy. He missed their nightly talks. He missed kissing and holding her. The longer he was away from her, the harder it was getting to stay away from her. Every time he would think to pick up the phone to call her, he would remember why they weren't together and he would get angry all over again. He couldn't stand the roller coaster ride. He knew that he would soon be taking another trip to Boston to finalize things with Turner. Duron offered to go in his place, not wanting his friend to come face to face again with Turner knowing that he would be marrying Victoria in a few months. Duron felt it would be hard on him, but Tyrone couldn't let him do that. Taija was too close to her due date for Duron to take any trips this late in her pregnancy, risking not being around if Taija needed him.

He would take the trip, deal with the business and take a return flight back out the same day. There was no need for him to hang around. As much as he missed Victoria, he didn't want to fall back into the same trap and be tempted to see her while he was there.

"Rack 'em up Ty. Let's get this game going," Duron said, breaking into his thoughts. He was glad Duron didn't bring up any conversation about Victoria. He wanted a night free of worry about what could have been with her. He needed this guy's night out.

~~

Turner called once again canceling dinner with Victoria. He informed her that he was very busy with something important and that he forgot Tyrone was coming into town to go over the re-designs they were working on.

As soon as Turner received his inheritance once they

married, he would then take over the family winery and he would begin the major plans for the expansion. She didn't have the heart to tell him that it may never take place because she wouldn't be marrying him. She hated to be the cause of him not receiving what was rightfully his. She only hoped that he could come up with a back-up plan. She would help him in any way she could, outside of marrying him. That was no longer an option.

She and Tyrone were meant to be together and she had every plan for that to happen, as long as he was agreeable.

Maybe his coming back to Boston was a sign. Victoria began feeling hopeful. Whether she had her heart to heart or not with Turner, she would tell Tyrone everything when he came to Boston. She couldn't imagine that he would come back to Boston and not at least call her. When he did, she would invite him over and tell him the whole truth and hoped that he would forgive her for making him feel like she didn't want him. She wanted him so much it hurt her to think of him and not be able to talk or see him. She would soon remedy that.

She was about to prepare herself some dinner when Taija called to check up on her.

"Hey girl," Victoria said when she answered.

"I was just checking up on you. How are things going?"

"Pretty much the same. I haven't had the chance to sit down and talk to Turner yet. He's had some business problems and we haven't been able to connect. Tomorrow Tyrone is scheduled to fly in to finish up some business with him so we won't get to talk tomorrow either. Either way, I'm telling Tyrone everything tomorrow. I'm sure he'll at least call me when he gets to town."

"It's one of the reasons I called. Duron mentioned

Tyrone was again flying out tomorrow to finalize the deal. My first thought was about whether or not you and Turner were able to talk so that you and Tyrone could finally talk things out."

"Well we haven't yet, but I'm not letting that stop me. Either way, this will be resolved this week. Enough is enough already," Victoria said.

"Well keep me posted and you know I'm here if you need me."

~~

Tyrone's plane landed and he was glad to see that the car Turner had sent for him had arrived. He was planning to go straight to Turner's office for the meeting and have the same driver take him back to the airport for his early return flight. The longer he stayed in Boston, the more he knew he would want to see Victoria. It was easier staying away from her when she was in another state. Being this close to her was going to be a task.

When he arrived at Turner's office, he was ushered right in for a quick chat before the meeting.

"Tyrone," Turner said greeting him with a handshake. "It's good to see you again. I'm looking forward to wrapping up the last few loose ends and finally getting these contracts signed. I'm looking forward to the work beginning in about nine months. When do you think you'd want to take a tour of the facilities in Washington?"

"The virtual tour you emailed me was great. Duron, Mike and I looked through that carefully, but yes I'd like to have an actual tour sometime in the next several weeks."

"Great, so let's make that happen. This is going to be a great partnership and all parties on my end are excited about the new plans."

"We're looking forward to the same," Tyrone replied, answering for the entire firm.

"Let's go over to my conference room. The rest of the team has already gathered."

Tyrone paused before following Turner.

"Turner, one thing. This comment has nothing to do with the business deal, but I wanted to tell you to cherish Victoria. Make sure that she is always number one in your life. There is nothing worse than a woman who doesn't feel like she's the priority. I'm not saying you're not treating her right. I'm only saying that I've experienced love and I wish I had a woman as wonderful as her. Now, on to business," Tyrone said. He watched as Turner seem perplexed by his comment. At least he'd said what he needed to say to hopefully give Turner a little advice and to also give himself some closure.

~~

Victoria kept checking the time, wondering if the business meeting between Turner and Tyrone was over yet. She was really hoping that Tyrone would either come by or call her. She purposely took the day off so that she could be available depending on when the meeting ended. Her heart skipped a beat when her doorbell rang late in the afternoon. She suspected that Tyrone had decided to just stop by, not giving her a chance to turn him away. She never would, but he wouldn't know that.

She ran to the door and opened it ready to leap into his arms when she was stopped in her tracks, seeing that it wasn't Tyrone at the door, but Turner instead.

"Turner, what are you doing here?" she said, looking around to see if Tyrone was with him.

"Well hello to you too," he said, coming inside. "I was

hoping we could finally talk."

"Sure," she said, feeling a little sad that it wasn't Tyrone at the door.

"Have a seat Victoria."

She took the seat on a chair across from him. She noticed he was nervous. This must be some discussion he wanted to have with her. She needed to talk to him as well.

"I'll tell you what. I know you needed to talk to me also, so why don't you go first," he said.

"Okay," she agreed.

"Turner, I can't marry you."

"What?" he replied being caught off guard. That's exactly what he was going to say to her, but he couldn't figure out how to start the conversation.

"I know this comes as a shock to you and I'm sorry. This puts you in a terrible bind and I didn't want that, but I'm in love with someone and I can't give up on that and marry you. I have to be able to see where this can go and marrying you would hurt any chance I may have at real love and happiness. She proceeded to tell a very stunned Turner the entire story of her affair with Tyrone.

"Turner, you don't seem upset. Did you hear everything I said?" she asked once she had laid it all out for him.

"Yes, I heard you. Victoria, I was coming over here to tell you the same thing; I can't marry you either."

Now it was Victoria's turn to be shocked.

"Okay, wait. Neither one of us wants to marry the other?" she asked.

"It seems that way," he replied calmly.

"Okay Turner, I see why I'm not nervous, cussing and screaming because I'm not in a position to lose a bucket load of money, but you on the other hand are. Why aren't you more upset?" she asked.

"I've met someone who happens to be the most incredible woman. I've been seeing her for a short time now and I am in love with her. This is not fake or made up like the engagement we have. I really am in love with her and we want to get married. I know you and I had all this planned out and never in my wildest dreams did I imagine that with my busy life, I would actually find real love. We fell in love almost instantly after we met. I've been keeping it from you because I wasn't sure how you would handle it especially after we've already told my family and your family. I didn't know how you would react when I dropped this on you. I didn't want any embarrassment coming your way with this. I didn't know how to deal with it. Her name is Cecily and you know her," Turner admitted.

"Is that the woman who interviewed us?" she asked.

"Yes it is."

"Were you already sleeping with her at that time?"

"No, it was not too long after that though; more like the same day actually, but later that night," he said with reservation. "Not before that."

"Turner, I'm happy for you," she said, meaning every word. "I'm in love as well. I have also been sort of seeing someone, or at least I was, that I'm madly in love with."

"Wait, you said was. What happened?" he asked.

"Well he sort of walked out on me. Let me give you the short version about that. I didn't tell you that part when I gave you the history. For starters, the guy I'm in love with is Tyrone Davis."

Victoria saw the look of shock on Turner's face at the mentioning of Tyrone's name.

"His last visit here to Boston things had gotten pretty

intense here at my house. Even after I told him I loved him and he told me he loved me as well, I still felt the need to protect you and I wouldn't tell him the whole story. He'd had enough of us sneaking around and he walked out on me. I haven't heard from him since that day," she confessed.

Victoria watched a shocked Turner who now sat with his mouth wide open, not believing what he was hearing.

"Wait, so after we got engaged, fake or not, you were rolling around in the sack having great sex while I was sitting at home like the good fiancé waiting for you to return to me?" he said, clearly kidding with her.

His humor about the situation made her smile.

"I'm glad we can laugh about this," she said. "Though things are rosy red in your world, that's not the case in mine. Tyrone asked me if I was willing to break things off with you to be with him and I told him no. I didn't want to say no, but I made a promise to you and I wanted to keep it. He caught me off guard and I hadn't had a chance to talk to you yet and I didn't want you to miss out on the opportunity to finally run your family's business and my saying no really screwed things up for me with him."

"Now something Tyrone said to me today makes a lot of sense. Earlier today, before I took him back to the airport, he gave me a little speech about being devoted to you and making sure I treat you right. It was as if he knew something, but didn't come out and say it."

"Wait, back to the airport? Tyrone's gone back to Atlanta already?" she asked.

"Yeah, he said he needed to get back to business so I drove him there myself before coming over here."

She couldn't believe he wouldn't even attempt to

connect with her. She did understand it though. She had hurt him and she needed to make it right.

She was hurt. She really hoped he would call her.

"So you and Cecily want to get married huh?" Victoria asked.

"Yeah. I told her all about you and she said that I was wrong for even suggesting that you give up a year of your life out of friendship."

"Turner, are you sure she's not doing all of this because you're about to be an even more wealthy man?" Victoria had to ask. She wouldn't be his friend if she didn't look out for him.

"Victoria, she comes from more money than me. Believe me, she is not after my money. She should be concerned I'm after hers," he said jokingly.

She got up to give him a hug.

"I'm happy for you. Just when you and I thought that we'd never find the one, we both did, at the same time."

"I'm happy for you too. Tyrone is a great guy and I think he's the perfect guy for you. I hope you have plans to make things right with him."

"I sure do and it's going to start with this weekend. I'm going to take a trip to Atlanta this weekend to pay him a visit and I'm not leaving until he accepts my apology and tells me again that he loves me. How are we going to handle things with our parents?" Victoria asked, knowing that her mom had already started working on wedding plans with Turner's mother.

"Don't worry about that. I'm taking Cecily home next week to meet my family and to explain everything to them. I'm also going to give your parents a call to explain everything to them as well as soon as I get home. I'll let you know when I have because I'm sure you'll want to talk to them right afterwards. I want to be the one to explain and apologize to them first."

She hugged him even tighter.

"You are the best friend in the whole world Turner. Cecily is lucky to have you. If she steps out of line though, I may have to take her out," she said, feeling glad that everything had been resolved and in a positive way. Well almost everything. She still needed to talk to Tyrone.

~~

Tyrone was back from Boston only a few days and already he regretted not seeing Victoria while he was there. He had come close a few times, to renting a car and staying an extra day to try and talk to her again. He also knew that Duron was right about not pressuring her. She needed to find her way to him and be willing to give up marrying Turner to be with him. Then and only then would he be ready to talk about their next steps.

It was Saturday and Duron's mother was expecting him for their chat. He showed up at Duron's parent's house right on time, at twelve noon. Ms. Barbara, Duron's mother had been standing at the door when he pulled up, no doubt ready to give him a tongue lashing if he had arrived even a minute late.

"Tyrone," she said, greeting him with a motherly hug when he came inside.

"Hey mom," he replied. She'd told him years ago to call her mom and he loved how it sounded.

"Come on in the kitchen. I was just finishing up a cake."

Tyrone could tell the minute he walked in the door that his favorite cake had been baked. She had made red velvet cake; his favorite.

"Sit down and I'll get you a piece," she said.

"How's Mr. Earl," Tyrone asked taking his seat, feeling like a little kid, anxious for a piece of cake.

"Oh, he's fine. He was due to be off today and work tomorrow, but we're babysitting Jake's kids tomorrow while he and his wife have a day together."

Tyrone knew that Duron's brother Jake was married to Kim and they had two kids, Milo and Lyric. He loved being around those kids. They were the first kids he had been around that made him long for kids of his own.

Tyrone watched as a plate was placed in front of him with a huge slice of cake of it. The plate had barely touched the table when he dug into it.

"So, my son seems to think you need to talk to me."

Tyrone looked up from the cake at her. He knew Duron had set up this little gathering. He also knew that if anyone would listen without judgment, it would be her.

"Yes ma'am. I think I do. It's about my mother," he said.

He watched as she took a seat across from him and settled in to let him vent.

"Okay, I have as long as you need son. Tell me what's going on and let me see if I can help," she said.

Tyrone already felt like a weight had been lifted as he went back to his childhood and told her everything he felt about his mother leaving him as a child.

Chapter 16

Victoria arrived in Atlanta Saturday afternoon and called Taija to let her know she was in town. She told her that if things didn't work out well with Tyrone that she'd take her up on the offer to stay at Duron's condo for the night since they never stayed there anymore. Taija told her she knew that things would work out and wished her well.

"I hope you're right about that Taija. I know I've hurt Tyrone in a way no one ever has. The first time he decides to give himself to one woman, that woman, me, doesn't choose him. I don't know what I was thinking. I love him so much and I plan to let him know that as soon as I talk to him. I will never give him room to doubt how much I love and want to be with him again."

"Why don't you come by the house and get the keys to the condo. I'm not saying things won't work out, but I want to be sure you have a place to stay no matter what. Plus I'll give you the address to his house. He never gives it out, but I know he wouldn't mind you having it."

"Okay, I'm on my way."

After saying hello and giving Taija a rundown of her

plan to win Tyrone's heart back, Victoria set out in the direction of Tyrone's house, using the address Taija had given her. She knew he lived in a very affluent part of Atlanta and was excited to see where he spent all of his time when not at the office. They had spoken on more than one occasion where Tyrone told her about his house and she could just picture it. She also knew of his love for cars and motorcycles and if things worked out and he forgave her, one of the first things she wanted to see was the garage he spoke so much about. She was a car lover herself and couldn't wait to see his collection. She put the address into her rental car's GPS to let it guide her.

~~

Heading to the office after his discussion with Duron's mother had Tyrone thinking of his next steps in handling the situation with his own mother.

He hadn't felt like driving out to his house and he knew he had a lot of work to catch up on. Only Ms. Barbara and his grandmother had the ability to get him to open up. Everything she'd said to him made sense as it pertained to how to handle his mother who wanted to be a part of his life after abandoning him as a child. He thought about her feedback on his situation on the drive to the office and realized her assessment was exactly what his grandmother was also trying to tell him.

He was being given a second chance to have a relationship with his own mother and he shouldn't waste it. It was true that his mother had made a grave mistake when he was young, but she was now trying to make amends and he should at least be open to giving her a second chance.

Having a better outlook on everything, he knew he needed to plan a visit to see his grandmother in the next week or so to try and connect with his mother. He would give an honest try to sitting down and listening to what she had to say.

He was glad Duron's mother had called him over to talk because he could always talk to her. It's times like those that he missed his grandmother the most. He could always call her on the phone, but the effect wasn't the same as talking to her in person. He admired Duron because of the closeness he shared with his parents. He never had that and he knew he was blessed that Duron's parents had always treated him as if he were one of their children.

He had been tempted to tell her about his issue with Victoria, but decided against it. She would have given him advice on how to fix it and at this point, he didn't want to fix it. He wanted to forget about her and though he didn't understand her decision to still marry Turner, he didn't want to pressure her into choosing between the two of them. He found it disturbing that women didn't know a good man and a good thing when it was presented to them all wrapped up in a big red bow like a sporty new car. He didn't need advice on how to fix his relationship. He needed something to take his mind completely off of his troubles. What he needed was a stress reliever and Vanessa, his no strings attached bed buddy was perfect for what he needed at the moment. He wasn't concentrating on work so before he thought too long and too hard about it, he picked up his office phone and called Vanessa to invite her over to his condo. He didn't stay at his condo often, but it was the only place he brought women to. None had ever been out to his house. It was his private domain, a place where he could escape from everything and everyone.

"Vanessa, hey it's Tyrone. Are you busy or did I catch you at a bad time?" he asked when she answered.

"Never too busy for you. It's been a while since I've heard from you," she said.

"You know how work can be for me. What are you doing tonight?" he asked, hoping she was free.

"If this call is what I think it is, then I'd say tonight I'm coming to visit you," she said.

"In that case, I'm at the condo. Call me when you get to the garage and I'll come down to get you."

"Sounds like a sexy plan to me. I have something new, black and lacey that I know you'll love. I'll see you in a few lover boy," Vanessa said, disconnecting the line.

Tyrone smile at the phone before placing it back on the receiver. If anyone could help him work on forgetting about Victoria, he knew it was Vanessa. This would help him get back to himself and forget about his troubles. He put away the papers he wasn't concentrating on anyway and made his way up to his condo to shower and change before Vanessa arrived.

~~

Victoria rang Tyrone's doorbell several times before realizing he wasn't at home. She checked the time and noticed that it was getting pretty late. As she headed back to her car, she called Taija to let her know she would be staying at Duron's condo for the night and would try Tyrone again in the morning.

"Did you try his cell?" Taija asked.

"I did and he isn't answering. I know he can see that it's me and he's probably still angry with me. I didn't leave a voicemail message because I really want to talk to him in person. I don't want him to realize I'm in town and avoid seeing me. I'll wait until tomorrow and perhaps he'll come into the office and I'll stop in there and see if he's in. Since I'll be at the condo anyway, I'm sure I'll run into him at the office in the morning. I was going to wait a while to see if he came home, but it's getting late."

"Okay, be careful and call me when you get to the condo and are locked in for the night. Tomorrow, some of Duron's family is coming over for a big dinner. Since I can't venture out, his mother is coming over here to cook so why don't you come by? If things work out with Tyrone, make sure he comes with you. If it doesn't, don't you dare let that keep you from coming, even if he'll be here too," Taija pleaded.

"Sounds great and no matter what happens, I wouldn't come all this way and not make time to spend with you and hear more about my soon coming godchildren. How are the babies by the way?"

"They are very busy these days. I need to keep them in for a few more weeks to be sure their lungs are fully developed and then I'm going to try and talk them into coming out. I can't wait until they get here. Duron says that will all change when they get here when lack of sleep sets in, but I don't care one single bit. I just want my babies born healthy and not too soon. We'll talk more tomorrow."

"Okay, I'll call you when I'm at the condo."

~~

Tyrone was making his way down in the elevator to ride back up with Vanessa and no matter how much he tried forgetting about Victoria, his mind just wouldn't let him. He had never met a woman before who was such a perfect match for him. It was apparent they were meant to be together. He couldn't imagine making the decision to be with someone out of obligation. He knew he would do anything for his friends, but there was always a place where a line should be drawn. He was disappointed Victoria couldn't see that.

As the elevator reached the garage level, he looked around for Vanessa's car. She flicked her car lights to let him know where she was parked. He watched as she stepped out of the car and the first thing he saw was her legs in very high stilettos, something that normally would start his anatomy wagging in anticipation, but that wasn't happening. Vanessa was a beautiful woman and she had legs that went on forever and his memory reminded him of the sweet spot that was at the juncture of those beautiful long legs. It was a spot that he'd sampled on numerous occasions and tonight would be a replay of that.

As he headed toward her car and she'd finally completely exited, he could see that she was already dressed for a night of fun. She knew how he loved seeing her in dresses that fit her body like a glove. She wore a dress just like that tonight, in bright red, wrapped at the waist, making it easy for him to remove it from her body and from his many nights of sinking into her, he knew she had a body that didn't quit. She was curvy and she knew exactly what to do with those curves to make his body hum. The anticipation of a wild night of sex with her always stirred his body. To his surprise, that wasn't happening. What was going on with him?

"Hey handsome," Vanessa said as he reached her.

"Hey yourself. You look beautiful."

"Thank you. Wait until you see what's under it just for you," she purred.

"I can only imagine," he said, trying to convince himself.

"I'm glad you called."

Vanessa shut her car door and headed toward her trunk for what Tyrone knew was probably an overnight bag. He reached for it before she could. He noticed she also had a larger suitcase in her trunk. He wondered what that was for.

Vanessa noticed the strange look on his face and looked to him to what could have caused his look. She realized he saw her even larger suitcase.

"I'm actually heading out of town in the morning. I have an early flight to Chicago for a business trip," she said moving closer toward him.

Tyrone knew that look in her eyes and knew that once they reached his condo, there would be no need for foreplay. He could read the signs. Normally he would be up for taking her wherever they were and knew that she would be down for it. For some reason, he was thinking too hard. His body had yet to react to the idea of being with her. He hadn't even greeted her with his normal kiss, the kind that would have her trying to crawl up his body and into his mouth. Maybe that was what was missing he thought as he turned back toward her as she followed him toward the elevator.

He turned around, let go of the suitcase and pulled her to him.

"I was waiting for this," Vanessa said, going willingly into his arms.

He focused on the bright red of her lips and couldn't wait to taste them. He went for her as she came forward toward him. Their lips met and they began a tongue duel that was familiar to them both. He tried to focus on the kiss and how good she felt in his arms, but nothing was happening like he expected. She was laying it on him thick like she truly missed him and was giving him a hint of what was in store once they reached the condo, but he still wasn't feeling it; his body still wasn't reacting to her. He tried to get as involved in the kiss as she was because he didn't want her to think he didn't desire her, so he continued reaching for that feeling he got when they kissed.

When the kiss broke off, he could sense that Vanessa knew something wasn't right.

"Is everything okay, Tyrone?" she asked.

"Yes, I'm just under a lot of stress. Let's go up to the condo where I'm sure we'll be a little more relaxed," he said grabbing the suitcase again. He saw a car about to park and when it pulled into a spot before reaching them, he guided Vanessa toward the elevator.

"I have just the thing to help you with that stress," she said seductively.

Tyrone knew she did and he was looking forward to it as they entered the elevator.

~~

Victoria couldn't believe her eyes. She had just pulled into the garage below the office park where Duron's condo was and was looking for a space near the elevator when she spotted a couple engaged in a kiss in the middle of the garage. She didn't want to honk her horn to get by so she sat and waited until they were done. The woman had on a hot, red dress and the sexiest heels Victoria had ever seen. The man's back was to her and even from the back he looked familiar.

She pulled a little closer and realized why the man, even from behind, looked familiar. He was dressed down in gray sweatpants, tennis and a navy long sleeved t-shirt, but she could never forget that body. The woman in the red dress was almost wrapped all the way around him as they engaged in a kiss that looked like they were familiar with each other. When they finally came up for air, Victoria could see that the man was Tyrone. She also took note that the woman came bearing a suitcase, apparent that she was planning to spend the night.

Victoria sat in her car stunned as her heart raced. She looked for Tyrone all evening so that they could talk and here he was at the office obviously about to entertain. They turned toward her after the kiss. She didn't want Tyrone to see her so she pulled into a spot right where she was. She watched out the side window as they proceeded, hand in hand toward the elevator. Victoria was crushed at the thought that Tyrone had already moved on.

There was no way she could stay at the condo now. She didn't dare run the chance of running into Tyrone and his guest since all of the condos were on the same floor. Victoria had no one to blame but herself. She should be the woman that Tyrone was walking with toward the elevator. She should be the one accompanying him to his condo for a night of magic that she knew the woman in red was about to experience. She knew what being with Tyrone was like and she missed it. She longed for it even more now that she'd seen him with another woman. It was a shock to her system actually seeing him with someone else and it hurt. She wanted to cry knowing that she had waited too long and Tyrone had already moved on to another woman.

She couldn't go back to Taija's house. She knew that she would have to explain what happened and she wasn't ready to do that. She pulled out her cell phone to call her.

"Hey Taija," she said when Taija answered on the first ring.

"I was waiting for your call. I was just about to call you. Are you settled in at the condo?"

"Yes," Victoria lied. "I am and I'm also more tired than I thought I would be so I'm going right to bed. I'll call you tomorrow," she added.

"Okay, but don't forget to let me know what happens with Tyrone and dinner is at seven tomorrow night."

"I won't. I'll see you tomorrow for dinner."

Victoria disconnected the call and pulled back out of the parking space. She would stay at a hotel for the night. She would think of something to tell Taija tomorrow. Maybe she would just tell her that she changed her mind about seeing Tyrone and thought it best for them both to just move on. She'd say that she thought all night about the whole situation and that was what she decided. She knew that with a group of people around, there wouldn't be time to really get into it and she would change her flight so that she could fly out right after dinner. She wouldn't have to worry about laying all the details out for Taija until she's had a chance to digest them herself. It was her own fault that she'd missed out on what was possibly the love of her life. She was sure she wouldn't be getting any sleep. She knew she wouldn't be able to take her mind off of the fact that Tyrone would be spending his night in the arms of another woman, making love to her and forgetting the name Victoria. As she drove off, tears fell down her cheeks, sad at how she messed everything up with Tyrone. One day she'd learn to get out of her own way.

Chapter 17

The next morning, Tyrone was back at his home just about to slide back under his latest car purchase when his cell rang. He was hesitant to check it at first. He didn't want it to be Victoria and then he also wanted it to be Victoria. He knew that she had called him a few times and he wasn't ready to speak to her yet. Just the sound of her voice would make him want her and if he was going to work at getting over her, he needed some distance, so he hadn't answered any of the times she'd called. He decided to not even check it. Whoever it was, he let the call roll over to voicemail.

When the ringing stopped, it rang again. It may be some kind of an emergency so he glanced at it. This time it was his grandmother calling and he answered immediately.

"Is everything okay?" he asked, forgetting to even say hello.

"Hello to you too and yes everything is just fine," his grandmother said.

"Did you just call?" Tyrone asked.

"No, this is my first call to you today. Is something

wrong Tyrone?" his grandmother asked with worry.

"No, not at all. My cell phone rang right before you called and I wasn't sure if that was you also."

"I just wanted to check on you. I know things with your mother are troubling and I wanted to say I'm sorry for pushing this on you when you weren't ready for it. She told me what happened when she showed up at your office. I didn't know she was planning to do that or I would have told her not to because I know you needed more time to think things over."

"Gram, it's okay. There is nothing to apologize for. I'm the one who should apologize to you. I know how much you care and bringing me and my mother together was not a horrible thing. I'm actually thinking of coming home for a few days soon and I'm open to sitting down with her to talk."

Tyrone could hear soft sobs coming through the phone. Hearing him say that he would give his mother a chance, he had no doubt, brought his grandmother tears of joy, not sadness.

"I'm so happy to hear that. It's been a long time and everyone deserves another chance, no matter what," she said.

He couldn't agree more. Her comment had many meanings behind it. He was ready to give his mother a chance to be a part of his life, at least in a small way to begin with. He also knew that he couldn't avoid talking to Victoria forever. She'd hurt him by the choices she'd made, but they needed to find a way to at least be friends. She was best friends with his best friend's wife so they had to figure out how to co-exist.

"I'll call you later this week Gram. I'm thinking I'll be

home next week for a few days. Can you let JoAnn know and see if she still wants to talk? I was pretty mean to her when she came to town." he asked. He called her by her first name, not being able to call her mother.

"Yes I will son and I know she understands your anger. How about I make all of your favorite dishes and the three of us can sit down to dinner? Would that be okay?"

"Yes, Gram I think that's perfect. I love you."

"I love you too son and thank you for being open to this. I think this will be good for us all. It's time to let the past be the past and look to the future while we all still have time."

"I agree Gram," he replied before hanging up.

Tyrone scrolled through the missed calls and noticed the previous call was from Duron and he'd left a message. Checking it, Duron had invited him over for a dinner they were having at his house that night. Tyrone had planned to work on his cars well into the night so he'd catch up with them another time. He needed time to himself to regroup.

~ ~

"Taija, why do you have that funny look on your face?" Duron asked with concern during dinner with his family. His parents stopped mid chew to look at Taija. His brother Jake and his wife and their kids were also at dinner and started to look as concerned as everyone else. His brother Brian was the only one who seemed to be pre-occupied and didn't notice that Taija looked odd. Victoria noticed as well and was the first up and out of her seat to come around to Taija along with Duron.

"Something's wrong," she said holding on to her stomach. Fear was clear on her face, matching the look on everyone else's face.

"Wrong how, baby? Talk to me," Duron said checking over her and looking to see if her water had broken.

Taija began to look ashen and everyone's level of worry went from three to ten.

"Duron, something doesn't feel right," she said looking at him with grave concern.

Duron didn't wait another minute before getting everyone into action.

"Brian, get my truck started. Jake, call the hospital and let them know we're coming in. Something's wrong with the babies," he said calm, yet nervous.

"Mom, call Taija's doctor. Her number is on the fridge," he said, glad that everyone was remaining calm, to not upset Taija even more.

Duron was able to get Taija up and in the truck and as his brother drove them quickly to the hospital, he said a silent prayer for his wife and the babies.

By the time they reached the hospital, which wasn't too long because Duron and Taija were not far from the hospital, Taija hadn't looked much better.

Victoria rode in the car with Jake and Brian, following behind Duron, Taija and his parents. Once they'd reached the hospital and had exited their cars, Taija was in full scream mode. Victoria assumed, like the rest of them that she was in premature labor. She hoped not because it was still too early for the babies to be born.

At the hospital, Victoria watched as things happened at the speed of light. When they arrived, Taija was immediately wheeled into the emergency room followed by Duron and his parents. His father made sure everyone at the hospital where he worked catered to his daughter-in-law with the best of care. The rest of the family, including

Victoria had been escorted to Duron's father's office to wait for an update on what was wrong with Taija.

Victoria watched as Brian paced back and forth. Jake wasn't on duty, but since he too was employed at the hospital, he left the area that they had been carted off to and went in search of answers. Before he had done so, he instructed Brian to call Mike and Loren in California to let them know they were at the hospital. He also told him at the same time to call Tyrone. He was family to them so he should know also.

That set Victoria's nerves even more on edge. She knew that as soon as Tyrone got the call, he would make his way to the hospital and he would know that she was in town. Just when she thought she wouldn't have to deal with him, she was about to come face to face with him. She knew that he would be on his way to the hospital as soon as he was told.

~~

Tyrone arrived at the hospital and asked the first nurse he saw how to get to the office of Dr. Earl Knight. He let her know that the family called because of an emergency and was told to meet them. The nurse got him a pass from the receptionist and gave him directions. When he reached the room, he saw Brian pacing back and forth in the hallway. He could see Jake through the glass window pacing inside the office. As he reached Brian, he inquired about the status of Taija and the babies.

"So far, we haven't gotten much of an update," Brian said.

Tyrone knew whatever was going on was serious.

"My dad stopped through to bring my mom in to sit down and relax in his office and all he said was that Taija had gone into pre-mature labor and they were trying to stop the contractions."

"How's Duron holding up?" Tyrone asked.

"He's doing good. He won't leave Taija's side."

"How is your mom? Can I get anybody anything?"

"My mom is a nervous wreck. Thanks, but Victoria went to get coffee and sandwiches for everyone from the canteen," Brian said.

Tyrone wasn't sure he'd heard him correctly.

"Wait, did you say Victoria?" he asked.

"Yeah, she was at dinner tonight at Duron's house when Taija went into labor unexpectedly."

"Really? Dinner? How long has she been in town?"

"I don't know," Brian said. "When I got to their house, she was there. I assumed she came into town to visit with Taija for a few days. Here she comes now," Brian said pointing beyond Tyrone.

Tyrone turned to see Victoria heading toward them.

"Hi," Tyrone said as Victoria reached them, smiled, nodded and kept walking into the office with Jake and Ms. Barbara.

It didn't escape Tyrone that Victoria didn't speak back. Things were pretty rocky between them and it really wasn't the time to get into a discussion of her being in town. He knew that she had called him several times, but hadn't left a message.

Tyrone left Brian standing in the hallway and went into the office to check on everyone else. He went first to Ms. Barbara and then shook hands with Jake.

"Thanks for having Brian call me, Jake. Any more word yet?"

"Just that they are trying to keep the babies in. They are

concerned about lung development at this point."

Jake then addressed his mother.

"Mom, Brian talked with Mike and Loren and they are taking the next flight here to Atlanta. I'll pick them up at the airport when they get here."

"Is it okay for Loren to travel by flight?" his mother asked.

"Yeah mom, she's fine to fly. She still has a little while to go yet and there is no danger to her flying at this point. You know we weren't going to be able to keep her away once we told her and as soon as she knew, there was no doubt she was going to want to be here for Duron and Taija. You know how she feels about Duron. He's always been her favorite," Jake said, adding a little humor to an intense room. He needed his mother to relax and not worry so much. He was glad when his mother smiled.

"You're right. Duron will be happy to see her. Jake, go find your father and see what's going on now," Ms. Barbara said.

When Jake headed off, Tyrone looked at Victoria who was also wracked with worry. She was so beautiful, even with worry lines. He went over to her.

"Victoria, I didn't know you were in town."

He was shocked at the look he received from her. Where her eyes were normally soft and inviting when he looked at them, what looked back at him now were eyes filled with anger and if he wasn't mistaken, hurt as well.

"My visit was unexpected," she said quietly, but sharply.

"I see," was all that Tyrone could think to say. She was clearly still upset with him for leaving Boston the way he did the last time they'd talked.

"So do I," Victoria replied before she thought it through.

"Do you think we could talk in private for a moment," he asked.

"I don't think right now is a good time for that Tyrone."

"Go ahead and talk," Ms. Barbara said. "If we get any update, I'll let you both know."

"I won't be far if you need anything," Victoria said to her before getting up. She followed Tyrone out into a quiet corner of the hallway.

"How have you been?" he asked when they were alone.

"Well, you would know that if you'd answered any of my calls," she said curtly.

"You're right and I'm sorry about that. Are you going to tell me how you've been now that we've gotten that out the way?" he asked.

"Not as good as you, apparently," she replied, a bit pissed off. She couldn't get the vision out of her head of him standing in the garage kissing another woman the night before. Jealousy was such a nasty beast and it was living inside of her at the moment.

"What does that mean? Why are you so upset with me? I'm not the one who chose to be with someone else when I'm clearly in love with another person," he quipped.

Victoria didn't immediately respond. Even though his words rang true, they still cut deep. She knew she had made a big mistake, but if he had picked up the phone even once, she would have explained to him the error of her decision.

"It doesn't matter now Tyrone, does it? Clearly you've moved on. If I didn't know that by the number of times you didn't answer my call, I know it now," she said, too angry at him and herself to even look him in the eyes.

"You're talking in circles. I've moved on? Moved on to

who?" he asked.

"Wait, is this the Tyrone I missed getting to know? The one who could be seen with another woman, yet not admit to it?"

He was perplexed, not sure what she was talking about. In his mind, she was talking in circles.

"Victoria, what are you talking about? What woman?" he asked.

"Tyrone I didn't come to town to visit with Taija, though I would have added that to my agenda. I came to talk to you."

"To me?" he asked. "When?"

"Yesterday. I flew in from Boston yesterday to talk to you to see if we could start over," she admitted, feeling frustrated that she was telling him everything as if it would make a difference. The visual of him with the woman in the garage was playing over and over in her head. She couldn't get rid of the sight of him kissing her.

"Victoria, I didn't know you had come to town to talk to me."

"Well that's obvious, again, something that could have been easily resolved if you had answered the phone when I called yesterday."

"I'm sorry about that. I was still angry and every time I saw your number all I could think about was you choosing to marry Turner even though you're in love with me."

Hearing that, Victoria tampered down her anger a little. She had no right to be angry with him. This mess was her fault, not his. Even though the circumstance that they were in being at the hospital was not the best, she decided to tell him what she came to Atlanta to tell him and get it over with.

"I realized you were right after you left Boston. I had a heart to heart with Turner and told him I couldn't go through with marrying him. I wanted to talk to you in person and explain everything to you. Taija had given me your address since every time I called you, you wouldn't answer the phone. I was determined though and I drove out to your house last night to talk to you, but you weren't there."

Tyrone knew he wasn't there. He had been at the condo. Thoughts of Vanessa ran through his mind.

"I actually stayed at my condo last night," he said, leaving out the part about Vanessa. He didn't think there was a need to bring that up.

"I found that out in a way I never wanted to."

"You found out what? I don't understand."

"Well, I understand. I don't want to talk about this anymore."

Victoria felt like crying remembering seeing another woman in his arms and remembering how she'd stayed up all night imagining what he and his guest were doing. She tried to walk around him, but he stopped her.

"Wait don't walk away. You came all this way to talk to me, so let's talk. This may not be the ideal situation to have this talk, but since you are here, let's talk this out."

Victoria gathered herself and nodded her head.

"Okay, now, do you want to tell me what's going on here? What did you find out in a way you never wanted to?" he asked.

Victoria held back the tears and continued on.

"I found out that you weren't at your house last night, but at your condo."

"I know, I just told you that."

"No, I knew before you told me."

"You knew how?" he prodded.

She took a moment to catch her breath before telling him what she saw. She looked up into his handsome face full of confusion.

"I saw you Tyrone."

The way she said those words made the hair on his arms stand at attention. The grave look on her face spoke volumes and he had a feeling he wasn't going to like where the conversation was going. He let her continue.

"After I couldn't reach you last night at your home, I was going to spend the night at Duron's condo. Taija had given me the passkey so that, depending on how things turned out with my talk with you last night, that I would have someplace to stay besides a hotel. I didn't want to stay at their house again, invading their privacy."

She took another deep breath before continuing. She hated saying the words, but she knew she had to get them out.

"I saw you last night in the garage with a woman in a red dress. I saw you kissing her and then I watched as the two of you got in the elevator that led to the condos. Like I said, after we split in Boston and you left to come back here and after last night, it was apparent to me that you were doing much better than I was. I came here because I felt like I couldn't live without you and I wanted to make things right. I was missing you so much and my plan was to come talk to you last night and lay everything out on the table. Little did I know that you had easily moved on from me, especially knowing that you said you were in love with me. It was that love that led me here to Atlanta. Boy was I sorry when I saw you last night," she said more angry with herself now than with him.

She had seen him, he thought to himself. Somehow, Victoria had seen him kissing Vanessa in the garage. From the look on her face, she had also been imagining what had occurred once they'd reached his condo. He needed to clear that up.

"Victoria, let me explain," he pleaded.

"There is nothing to explain. It's okay and after what I took you through, I deserved that. After what I've been doing, leading you on and not being able to follow through, I deserved to see that. I wish you all the luck with whoever that was you were with last night. That looked like some kiss," she said, finally breaking away and going around him. She didn't want anyone to see her upset so she didn't go back into the room to wait with the family. She needed to walk it off so she headed for the elevator to get some air outside. She needed a moment to gather herself and come back in a better state to support the family. Her own personal problems needed to take a back seat.

Tyrone started to stop Victoria from walking away, but he knew she needed a breather. He was stunned that she had seen him last night with Vanessa in the garage. He wanted to tell her that what she saw was nothing, but he remembered that kiss and from someone on the outside looking in, it did look like a lot, but it really wasn't. He would give her time to regroup and they would talk again. There was no way was she leaving Atlanta after she'd come all this way to talk to him, and not really have a heart to heart. He had to explain to her the events of the night before. If after that, she still wanted to walk away, he would let her. It would be hard, but he would let her. He still wanted her, he still loved her and what she'd witness last night had been a mistake. Inviting Vanessa over was a mistake he now regretted more than anything. Luckily it was the only mistake he'd made last night that he felt regret over. The night could have turned out differently and he could have been in a worse position than where he currently was. He hoped his conversation with her later would clear everything up. He headed back into the room at the same time that Duron showed up to give everyone an update.

Just as Duron was about to speak, Tyrone saw that Victoria had slipped back into the room to join him, Jake, Brian and Duron's parents.

"Taija is doing much better. She was in fact in premature labor and they were able to stop the contractions for now. She's being thoroughly examined, but her doctor thinks that if in fact they can't continue to stop the contractions and if the lives of the babies or Taija are in danger, that she could deliver them and the hospital will give them the care they need to survive. We'll cross that bridge when we get to it. I talked with Taija's mother briefly and she's flying in tonight. She wanted to catch a cab from the airport, but I'm sending a car to pick her up. Dad's assistant is here tonight and she's agreed to keep an eye out for her and bring her here when she arrives. I think it's going to be a long night. I'm going back into the room with Taija and as soon as they allow visitors, each of you can see her one at a time. Jake, if you need to leave I understand."

"I'm good bro. Kim took the kids home and I told her to call me if she needed me, otherwise, I'd be here until I knew Taija and the babies were okay."

Duron looked at Tyrone.

"Don't even think about it bro. I'm not going anywhere," Tyrone said.

"Thanks everyone. Victoria, I told her you were still here also. As soon as I can, I'll get you in to see her. Taija said you had a flight back home in about an hour."

Tyrone looked at Victoria hoping he didn't hear what he thought Duron had said, that she would be leaving to return to Boston within the hour.

"Thanks Duron. I did have a flight, but I cancelled it. I'm not leaving until I know she's alright. Do you mind if I stay a few more nights at the condo?" she asked.

"Not at all. Stay there as long as you like."

Tyrone was glad to hear that Victoria would be staying. That would give him more time to talk to her. It bothered him to think that Victoria may have been in the condo next to his the night before after seeing him with Vanessa in the parking garage. What that must have done to her ate at him. He was hoping he could talk to her much sooner than later. He didn't want her going on with thoughts running through her head of what she thought he may have been doing last night.

"Okay, well I'm going back in with Taija. Thanks everyone for being here," Duron said.

CHAPTER 18

Everyone was elated that Taija was doing much better since she'd made it through the night without any more contractions.

"Now that we know everything with Taija and the babies is going to be fine, do you want me to drop you off at the condo on my way home?" Tyrone asked Victoria. He was hoping for another chance to talk to her even it was in the car ride back to the condo.

None of them had left since arriving with Taija the night before. She was resting well and the doctors were keeping an eye on any stress on Taija or the babies. He suggested everyone go home and get some rest and he would call if anything changed.

Victoria didn't really want to leave, but she was tired and she could use a nice long, hot bath.

"Sure, I would appreciate that."

They hadn't talked anymore throughout the night, keeping their personal problems on the back burner while they focused on being support for the family.

"I'm ready when you are. I'm planning to go home to get a shower and come back after grabbing some clothes for Duron so that he can change without having to leave the hospital."

"Actually my rental is at Taija's house. If you can drop me by their house to get it, that would be fine since you have to stop their anyway. I can then drive myself to the condo."

"Okay," Tyrone said walking with her to the garage after saying their goodbyes to everyone. They had all agreed to meet back at the hospital after a few hours of sleep.

They rode in silence for most of the ride to Duron and Taija's house. Tyrone noticed that Victoria looked out of the car window the entire time, never looking in his direction. He had a feeling that the scene in the garage was playing through his mind.

Every time Victoria looked at Tyrone, all she saw was him locking lips with the woman in red in the garage. She couldn't get the vision out of her head. Those lips that brought her so much pleasure were locked with another woman's and clearly he had enjoyed it. She didn't know what to say even though they were alone in his car.

"Victoria, we need to talk. The silence between us is killing me and it's killing me knowing you saw me the other night. You came all this way to talk to me and I think we should get it all out."

She turned her body around and looked at him.

"That was before I realized you were already seeing someone else. I guess I should have expected that. I never thought you'd be pining away for me here in Atlanta. I admit I wasn't expecting to see what I saw the other night," she confessed.

"I can explain about that night if you let me," he said.

"No need to explain Tyrone. I may not like it, but I do understand."

Tyrone knew he had to fix this and not let her leave town with this issue between them.

"Ride out to my house with me and let me cook you breakfast. We can talk and then I'll take you to get your car so that you can go back to the condo. I really want to talk first."

"Okay," Victoria replied. She saw no harm in that and if he had an explanation, she would let him get it out.

He turned the car around and headed in the direction of his house.

Victoria was nervous as Tyrone escorted her into his house through the garage.

"Is this the car you told me you were getting? It's a beauty," she said admiring the sleek shiny car.

"Yes it is. I still have a lot more I want to do on it. I'm glad you like it since I know you love cars as much as I do. Come on inside and let me get you something to eat. I'm thinking omelets. Is that good with you?"

"Yes, I love omelets."

"Yes, I know. You told me during one of our many late night conversations. How about you cut up some fruit while I slice up ingredients for the omelet."

They watched each other as they moved around his kitchen. He gave her instructions on where she could find everything she needed and he went in search of everything he needed. He was glad that for the moment, the sad look that had been on Victoria's face had disappeared as she took to task the job of helping him prepare breakfast.

"This kitchen is gorgeous. This is a kitchen any chef

would love," Victoria said looking around at all of the stainless steel appliances and cookery that any master chef would admire.

"I love to cook and the one thing I wanted when I built this house was a grand kitchen."

Victoria smiled at him and for a moment, the things that tore them apart were no longer a cloud hanging over them.

"Can I get you some coffee?" he asked, moving around the kitchen.

"Coffee would be a blessing right now after being up all night."

He got the coffee maker going while grabbing the rest of the items they would need for breakfast from the fridge.

Victoria continued to admire the magnificence of his kitchen. She was sure the rest of his house was just as nice. When she had pulled up to the house the night before, she had no idea it would be this huge inside. For just one man, the house was large. This house could fit three houses the size of hers in it. It was not only large and spacious, from what she could see, but it was spectacular. She wondered if Loren had also decorated his home. She knew that Loren had done Duron's home and his condo as well as the condo for Mike and Tyrone at the office park. If this was her touch on his house, Victoria thought that maybe she could get some tips from her on brightening up her own house.

While she sliced fruit and Tyrone put together all the items to make the omelets, she figured now was as good a time as any to talk. Being around him again had diminished the jealousy and anger she had felt toward him the night before. She had no right to be jealous.

"So, are we going to talk now?" Tyrone asked before she could.

"Yes," she answered. "I know you want to explain last night to me, but let me say some things first."

"Okay," he said.

Victoria hesitated trying to decide how to tell him the whole story. She decided to start with something easy. She sat the utensils down on the counter where she'd been prepping the fruit and turned her full attention on him.

"I've missed you," she said. She watched as her words caused no reaction from him. "I wanted you to know that before I said anything else."

"I've missed you too, but that doesn't fix things Victoria."

"I know and I'm hoping you'll hear me out. I want to tell you everything. Are you open to hearing it?" she said.

"Absolutely, but before you do, let me clear something up about last night, okay?" he asked. "I want to be sure the air is clear about that first, so let me get that out of the way."

Victoria nodded in the affirmative.

"I know what you saw last night in the garage, but nothing else happened and I mean that; nothing. Of course, nothing happening was not the plan, but that's how it turned out. After we got to the condo, I couldn't go through with it. For the first time in my life, I couldn't go forward with getting a woman into my bed. I had originally called Vanessa, that's the woman you saw, because I wanted anything that would help me get over you. I was crushed when you decided to stay with Turner. For years I avoided any type of serious relationship and when I thought that I had finally found the one woman that I wanted to make a go at a relationship with, it turns out that she's engaged to marry someone else. After a few minutes of being at the condo, even Vanessa could tell that something was different. She was someone that I had a no-strings type of situation with. We talked for a while and she told me that I shouldn't give up on you and the kind of happiness I had found since I'd met you. She wasn't there for more than an hour before she left. I hope you believe me when I tell you, other than the kiss you saw, nothing else happened. After she left I got some work done and went to bed. I got up early, came here and was doing some work on my car until I got the call from Brian about Taija."

Victoria was glad to hear that nothing happened between Tyrone and the woman he was with. Now maybe she could get her imagination to stop messing with her about what she thought happen between him and the woman.

"I'm glad to hear that. You have no idea the things that have been going on in my head since I saw you two. I have never been that jealous in my life. I was never really angry, just disappointed that if it hadn't been for me, that could have been me with you last night and you wouldn't have felt the need to replace me with someone else."

"I think I've discovered that's not possible. Clearly that night proved that to me."

"Okay, my turn," she said.

"I'm not engaged to Turner anymore. I was, but it wasn't a real engagement. Turner and I have been friends since childhood, something I know I told you about. We are actually best friends. He stood to inherit a lot of money and to take over as chief executive officer of the family winery business. There was a stipulation that involved him having to be married in order to get it."

Tyrone couldn't believe what he was hearing. Families

still did that? What century were they living in?

"I can see it all over your face. Yes, it's crazy, I know, but yes, old families with big money still do things like that. That stipulation was put in place by Turner's grandfather because he didn't want any philandering in the top position. He wanted Turner to be settled down, living as a family man to keep the image of the company intact. I agreed, as his friend, to marry him to fulfill the requirements for his inheritance and in a year we would divorce. I couldn't tell anyone, not even Taija because it was important that we kept the façade in place so that nothing would affect his getting what was rightfully his. For years, like me with men, Turner felt that the perfect woman for him didn't exist. Being each other's best friend, we knew all about each other's dating lives and it was bad," she laughed. It felt good getting it all out once and for all to Tyrone.

"Since neither of us were seriously dating anyone, I agreed to do this for him. Who knew that I would then fall in love with you. I wanted to do the right thing and I didn't want him to lose everything. I finally told Taija about everything after you'd left Boston because I was so distraught. She told me that I shouldn't give up on what I wanted in order to help anyone, including Turner. I was entitled to a life too; especially a life with a man that I dreamed of being with. You are my everything, Tyrone and I'm sorry for all this mess I've caused."

Tyrone was shocked at what he was hearing and felt the need to take a seat while she continued. He had a feeling the story was about to get even better.

"After I decided to talk to Turner to tell him I couldn't go through with the marriage because I was in love with you and I didn't want to lose you, he told me that he had met someone as well and was keeping it a secret from me."

Tyrone assumed that was the woman he had seen Turner with.

Victoria thought that after all she'd already said that Tyrone would have something to say or at least have a few questions for her. She watched and saw no reaction cross his face.

"Are you going to say something?" she asked after telling him the entire truth. He hadn't spoken the whole time while she spilled on everything that had happened from the moment Turner had thought up the idea of the engagement and marriage so that he wouldn't lose his inheritance or his chance to take over the family business.

She watched as he continued to stare at her without speaking. She was about to ask him again when he got up, came around to her side of the island, turned her around so that she was facing him and without words being spoken, he let her know what he'd thought of what she'd just said.

He caught her face between both of his hands and pulled her face into his for a kiss.

He kissed her like a starving man. He kissed her for all the time they'd spent apart. He kissed her for every night he'd gone to bed dreaming about her. He wanted her to feel in his kiss that he still loved her just as much as he did the first time he'd said it. Nothing had changed for him other than the fact that he realized he no longer had to hide his feelings for her anymore from anyone.

"I love your mouth Victoria. I think it was meant just for me," he said pulling back before going back in for another kiss. He couldn't get enough of her. The way she was holding on to him and joining him in the kiss let him know that she felt the same way.

They were both out of breath by the time they pulled away from each other. Neither really wanted to, but they were still talking and needed to get everything out on the table.

"So you weren't in love with Turner?" he asked, happily.

"I love him, yes, because he is my best friend, but I'm not in love with him, no. The only man I'm in love with like that is you."

Tyrone kissed her again and again and again as if he needed to kiss her just to breathe.

Victoria smiled after they broke off the kiss again.

"Does this mean you forgive me?" she asked.

"Baby, there is nothing to forgive. I love you and now I know that this was something you needed to work out. I was always going to be here. I've been waiting on you even though I was angry. I'm glad it didn't take you a lifetime to figure out what you needed to do."

Victoria was happier at this very moment than she thought she would ever be.

"I love you too, Tyrone. It feels so good to say that to you again. I hope you won't ever tire of hearing me say it," she said cheerfully, overwhelmed by how happy she was.

"Say it as often as you like as long as you never tire of hearing me say it to you," he said.

"Never," she exclaimed loudly.

"So, is there anything else that needs to be cleared up?" he asked.

"I'm all tapped out," she said. That's what I came all this way to tell you. What about you? Anything else you want to tell me?" she inquired.

"Nothing except that I love you," he said backing up out

of the kitchen bringing her along with him.

"I thought we were going to eat," she said.

"Food is not what I'm starving at the moment."

Victoria could look in his eyes to see he had other plans besides cooking.

"I thought I'd give you a tour of my house, starting with the bedroom. I think you'll love it," he said.

Not giving her a chance to reply, he lifted her up into his arms and carried her up the winding staircase that led to his bedroom.

"Some tour," she said. "Everything is passing by me in a blur you're moving so fast," she chuckled at his hurriedness to get her to the bedroom.

"We'll check out all of the other rooms one by one. I have a different position in mind for each of them. Right now the only thing I need is you, naked. I've missed you and I want to show you how much."

Victoria couldn't agree more.

Once they reached his bedroom, Victoria barely had time to take in the magnificence of the space. His bedroom was huge. Everything was all masculine in shades of gray and black. She assumed because of his height, he had the biggest bed she'd ever seen. It was long to accommodate his size and wide enough for them to spend the day rolling around it in and not falling off.

Tyrone didn't take the time to set Victoria down when he reached his room. He went straight for the bed. Instead of laying her on it, he stood her up on it. Because of how high his bed was, when he stood her on it, he was face to face with that part of her that he'd missed tasting and plunging inside of. He was a man on a mission and his mission, and he chose to accept it, was to get her out of every stitch of clothing as fast as he could. There was no time for pleasantries. They had already wasted weeks apart. He didn't want to waste any more time.

He reached down to first remove Victoria's shoes. Those were immediately joined on the floor by her pants and top, leaving her standing on his bed in a royal blue demi cup bra and royal blue satin and lace high cut panties. Just the kind he liked, he thought. Before he divested her of her panties, he placed his nose at the center of her essence and drew in her scent, familiarizing himself once again.

He could tell that Victoria was as turned on as he was. He could hear her shallow breathing as she tried to suppress the need to jump him.

This time Victoria would let him take from her what he needed. The times they had been together, he had always allowed her to take what she needed and get from him what she wanted. Now she just wanted to delight in his feel and his touch.

She was caught off guard when he slowly slid her panties to the side and settled his mouth over her center going in for that nub that was peeking at him, waiting for attention. She closed her eyes and threw back her head the minute he grabbed on to it lightly with his teeth. The pressure felt incredible. Victoria didn't think she'd last long. Tyrone continued to pleasure her as she stood on his bed, holding on to his shoulders. She felt his hands as they widened her stance allowing him even more and greater access to bring her pleasure. Her body, on its own was grinding into his mouth. She couldn't stop the action even if she tried and she wasn't planning to. Her mind went crazy with want as he went in for the kill. He was now using his tongue and his fingers to give her what she needed, while also giving himself what he needed and wanted.

Tyrone needed her taste. He loved how she was so cleanly shaved that his tongued glided over what felt like silk to him. He heard her moan loudly and without restraint as he continued with his tongue assault while reaching up to squeeze her nipples that were standing at full attention. The combined assault did the job.

He lapped at her like it was his last meal as she came over and over and over. He didn't let up even when she tried to pull away. He moved his hands down from her breasts, around to cup her round, plump behind to keep her in place. He rocked with her as she rocketed through one orgasm while another came crashing down on her immediately after the first.

Victoria couldn't stand on her weak legs anymore. She collapsed first into Tyrone and then back on the bed as he laid her down. Before she had a chance to even think, he had removed all of his clothing and was donning a condom when she looked up to see he was joining her on the bed.

"I wanted to taste you too baby," she said, sexily, with a glow of a thoroughly satisfied woman.

"Next time baby. I've waited too long to be inside of you and I don't want to wait any longer."

Victoria had barely caught her breath when she felt Tyrone slide into the apex of her thighs. As soon as she felt his tongue enter her mouth, his hard, throbbing flesh entered her body.

Tyrone lifted Victoria's legs high to where her knees were almost next to her head.

Victoria knew in her mind that her body was in for

something good. This appeared to not be one of those slow, sexy moments. He needed her and he needed her hard and deep. This position would give him the deep penetration he wanted more than he wanted his next breath. Victoria knew she would give him anything he needed and wanted as long as he never stopped making her feel good. She always felt cherished, wanted and loved with him and she couldn't believe she'd almost lost him.

"I won't hurt you, baby," he whispered in her ear as he placed his head in the space between her head, her shoulder and her leg which was now all the way up on the side of his head.

"I know you won't. Get what you need baby, I want it too," she said ready for the intensity of his love making. He didn't disappoint.

Tyrone's mind was clouded with nothing but how Victoria felt wrapped around him. He wanted to go slow and make it last, but he needed her with a fierceness that he didn't know existed. He kept his head down next to her face as he continued to whisper his love for her while at the same time telling her in very explicit terms what it felt like to be inside of her like this again. His words were not only driving him to pump into her harder and faster, but they were also causing her to meet him stroke for stroke. She wanted everything he was giving her.

Where Victoria thought there may be discomfort because of how high her legs were up, she loved the feeling. She wanted him to know that her love for him was boundless and she was open to giving him what he needed from her. This was about what he wanted and right now, he wanted her badly. He was pounding into her like a madman, screaming her name over and over again as if he couldn't believe she was back in bed with him again.

Victoria could cry at the emotions flowing through her. She loved him so much and the thought that she could have missed out on being with him like this again caused another orgasm to erupt, followed by Tyrone's own release. The impact of how ravenous he was for her triggered another release from her that stole her ability to breathe. She couldn't even scream. She was hungry for him as she reach her arms around to grab around his muscular back and held on for the rough, yet pleasurable ride. She needed this as much as he did.

Tyrone rode her hard as he rode out wave after wave of his orgasm. He never stopped his relentless plunges into her soft, supple womanhood until all signs of his release had begun to subside. As he slowed his thrusts, not stopping them, he released her legs and rubbed his hands up and down her body as if he was checking to be sure she was real.

"I love you baby," he said, realizing the impact of the fact that they were together again and they no longer had to sneak around.

"I love you too baby."

"I love you so much. Thank you for coming to me," he said, meaning every word as he placed kissed along her neck and jawline before taking her mouth in a kiss that let her know once again that she was his.

"Thank you for accepting me even after what I put you through. I'm never, ever leaving you again," she said.

"Never," was the last thing Tyrone heard before he and Victoria both slipped into a deep slumber. They were not only tired from the lack of sleep or from the intensity of their love making, but from the exhaustion of the pain of being apart from each other.

A little while later, somewhere a phone was ringing, Victoria thought as she tried to come awake. Her slumber was so deep after the love she had shared with Tyrone, she didn't know if the ringing phone was a dream or not. Making love with Tyrone had surpassed any other time they'd been together. Now that they decided to give a real relationship a try, Victoria was hoping her body would survive sex between them getting better and better.

She slowly opened her eyes, again, aware that a phone was still ringing and it sounded like hers. She looked over to see that Tyrone was still sound asleep.

She tried not to wake him as she got out of bed to catch her phone before it went to voicemail. She followed the sound to her pants that were on the floor near a chair, having landed there when Tyrone took them off. It stopped ringing just as she reached it. She was about to turn around to join Tyrone in bed when the ringing started again. She grabbed for it without looking at who was calling.

"Hello?" she said wondering who was calling so early in the morning.

"Victoria, it's Turner. I didn't hear back from you and I stopped by your place this morning and got no answer."

She took a few moments to make sure she was fully awake.

"I'm fine Turner and I'm still in Atlanta. Taija went into premature labor yesterday. I'll be back in a few days."

"How did things go with Tyrone?" he asked.

"Everything is fine. Listen, I can't talk right now. I'll call you later."

"Oh, I get it. You and Tyrone are still sleeping I take it?"

he said with a chuckle.

"Bye Turner. We'll talk later."

She disconnected the call and felt two strong arms encase her and it felt good to be in his arms again. She moaned as she fell into his embrace.

"Good morning or is it afternoon?" he said, placing kissing all across the back of her neck. Victoria tried to turn around to face him and get a real kiss, but he wasn't having any of that."

"Oh no you don't," he said whispering in between kisses.

"I want a real kiss," Victoria said.

"Mmmm and I want you just like this," he crooned with desire.

Victoria melted back in to him. She knew she couldn't deny him anything. She was right where she was supposed to be and wanted to be. The next sound she heard was that of him opening up a condom packet. She melted at the feel of him as he moved up closer behind her, seeking entrance once again into her body, feeling that he was again hard as steel and searching for a way in.

"Let me in baby," he said, moving her to lean against the dresser along the wall and lifting her leg up to prepare her for his entry. She loved that he was all about different positions.

She pushed back further into him as she held her leg up, waiting for that feeling that always came when he took her. She gasped when she felt his fingers first part her swollen lips surrounding her sensitized nub and then the head of him, thick and wide sought entry. He didn't enter her all the way, but used short pumps to be sure she was wet and ready for him. It didn't take her long to get there.

"Oh, you are ready for me I see," he said, realizing his

fingers were now drenched with her wetness and he easily slipped in. This time they did it in slow motion, him going in and out at a much slower pace than before, but still just as powerful and arousing.

It didn't matter if they were hard, fast and wild with abandonment or slow and seductive, they felt the buildup that they knew would soon send them over the edge and into that happy abyss.

A short time later, Tyrone called Duron to check on Taija. He and Victoria had finally made their way down to the kitchen to eat and he wanted to get the latest. No one had called so he assumed everything was the same as it had been when they'd left the hospital hours ago.

He was confused when Mike answered Duron's phone.

"Mike? What's going on? Why are you answering Duron's phone?"

"Hey Ty. His phone has been ringing off the hook with friends who heard that Taija was in the hospital so I'm playing secretary today. I was actually just about to call you."

"Cool, how's Taija doing?"

"She's doing good. You may want to make your way here to the hospital. We just got the word that they are going to have to take the babies out soon. There is no need to be alarmed. The doctors feel it's best and they are sure the babies and Taija will pull through just fine. Do you have a number for Victoria? Duron said she's still here," Mike said.

"Actually she's with me. I'll tell her and bring her with me."

"Ah, that's good to hear. I take it things have worked themselves out between you two? Duron gave me the rundown on everything."

"Yeah, things have worked out very well. We'll talk later. Tell Duron I'm on my way and I'll bring Victoria. I'll stop at his house to get him some clean clothes to bring with me. How's Loren?"

"She's fine. You know she was a worry wart until she laid eyes on Duron and saw that everything was okay."

"I'm sure. Tell her I said hello and we'll see you in a few," he said hanging up and getting up to find Victoria who was in the shower. She exited just as he'd entered the bathroom.

Her smile disappeared the moment she looked into his eyes. Something was wrong.

"What is it?" she asked.

"Mike called. They are preparing to deliver the babies."

Victoria looked like she was about to panic..

"Don't worry so much. Taija is getting the best care and her doctor is doing what I'm sure is best for all of them. Why don't you get dressed and let's head over to the hospital."

Victoria didn't answer. She rushed to get dressed.

After stopping at Duron's house, they headed straight for the hospital to find that Taija was in the operating room where they were about to deliver the babies. Everyone gathered in one room to have prayer and to wait. There wasn't much talking, but there was a lot of pacing back and forth until finally Duron came into the room smiling. Everyone exhaled knowing his smile meant good news.

"We have two new members of the family. They are doing really well. They were taken to the neonatal unit, but the doctors all say they are optimistic that they'll both be fine. Taija is doing well and was a trooper throughout the delivery. She'll be a while before they put her into a room, but she's fine. Of course she's worried about the babies. She only got the chance to see both of them briefly before they were whisked away. They are the cutest little babies I've ever seen and I'm not just saying that because they are mine."

Everyone hugged and congratulated Duron.

"Wait," he said. "I forgot I took pictures of them before they were taken away."

Duron showed off pictures of his children.

"Let me introduce you all to Autumn and Brent Knight, my baby girl and baby boy."

Duron flipped through several pictures of the babies before going back to check on them and Taija.

Now that everyone could exhale there was chatter where there had been silence laced with worry.

"I'm glad Taija and the babies are okay. They are the cutest babies I've ever seen," Victoria said. Everyone agreed with her and then decided that as soon as they were able to see Taija they would all go home to get some much needed rest. It would be at least a day before they would be able to get a glimpse of the babies in the pediatric unit.

Victoria watched Tyrone as he and Mike talked about how happy Duron was and how happy they were for him that everything had worked out. Everyone had been scared, not knowing what would happen. Now she could focus on the fact that she and Tyrone were a couple and no one around them seemed to be surprised to see them together.

"Second cutest to the one's we'll have one day," Tyrone said, surprising her.

She turned around toward him, not sure she'd heard him correctly. Apparently she wasn't the only one who'd heard him. Where there was chatter, there was once again silence. She looked around and everyone was smiling at her and Tyrone.

"Well it's about time," Mike said.

"Yes!" Loren exclaimed from her seat with her hands resting on her own growing belly.

"Why don't we go grab some coffee for everyone while we wait to be told we can see Taija," Tyrone said, going over to walk Victoria out with him before she passes out from embarrassment. It was obvious more people in the room knew that something was going on between them than they thought.

"Now that the worst with Taija has passed, I'm assuming someone in this room will tell me what the secret is with Tyrone and Victoria while they're gone," Tyrone heard Duron's mother say, smiling at him.

"I love this family," he said as he shook his head and walked out with Victoria.

Chapter 19

It was late at night and Tyrone and Victoria had finally made it back to his house after visiting the hospital and checking out their new god-daughter Autumn and their new god-son Brent. After visiting with Taija and the twins, they finally shared with everyone the news that they were a couple who were happily in love. After returning with coffee and getting many stares, they knew they weren't going to be able to leave the hospital without telling them what was going on.

They left out the information about the fake engagement between Turner and Victoria, but they did let everyone know that her relationship with Turner was over and that they were in love. After getting over the initial shock of hearing Tyrone say he was in love with someone, everyone congratulated them on the love that was evident every time they looked at each other.

Now they were settling in at his house realizing that soon she would have to return to her life in Boston, something that didn't sit well with him. Now that they were officially together, he didn't want distance keeping them apart. If things went the way he was planning, he wouldn't have to deal with distance for much longer.

As soon as he joined Victoria on the sofa in his media room, she turned around to him with a questionable look.

"What did you mean by what you said at the hospital?" she asked.

"What did I say?"

"When we were all saying how cute the twins were, you said something about them being second cutest to the one's we'll have one day. Did you mean that?"

"Yes I meant it. I loved the look of pure shock and awe on your face when I said it. I looked just like the one on your face right now," he said.

"We're having babies one day?" she said.

"Victoria, we are together sweetheart. I have no plans of ever letting you go again. I know you have to get back to Boston to work, but I don't want you to go back wondering what will happen with our relationship when you do. I love you and I want you to be my wife."

Before she could take in what he was saying, she watch him pull a ring box out of his pocket and place it in the center of his palm, holding it out for her to take. When she was about to reach for it he stopped her.

"Before you open this box I want you to know that since the first day I laid eyes on you, you've taken my breath away. After spending time getting to know you and being with you, I can't go another day without making sure that you know how I feel about you. We've been on this rocky road from the start and I'm happy that's over with. Now it's time to move to the next level and not waste any more time. I love you and I want you to be my wife Victoria Denise Alston. Say you'll marry me?"

With shaky hands, Victoria opened the box and saw a gorgeous marquee shaped diamond and platinum engagement ring staring back at her. When did he have time to buy a ring, she thought. They had been together since she first saw him at the hospital.

"When did you have time to buy a ring?" she asked, curiously.

"I called my jeweler this morning when you were still sleeping and I told him what I wanted. I knew without a doubt that before you left Atlanta, I was going to ask you to marry me so that when you left, you would never have a doubt about our commitment to each other. I'm all in baby," he said.

He watched as tears streamed down her face, not of sadness, but of pure delight.

"Tyrone, nothing in this world would make me happier than being your wife. You are the man I have dreamed of my whole life. From that first moment in Texas when I sat across the table from you, you blew me away. I never stopped thinking about you from that moment forward. I didn't realize what a huge mistake I was making going along with the marriage plan with Turner until I'd met you. I didn't want a fake marriage of any kind. I knew that if I were ever going to be married, I'd want it to be with a man who is loving and kind and who makes me feel like I'm the most beautiful woman in the world. I don't know how to explain it, but after that first night, after having dinner and making love with you, I knew that we were the perfect combination. It was also ironic that when I got to the airport and I sat down to relax before the flight, I put my IPod on to shuffle some nice music and the first song was "Perfect Combination" by Stacy Lattisaw and Johnny Gill.

Yes, I will marry you baby. There is nothing more that I could ever want in my life than to call you my husband," she said before Tyrone removed the ring from the box and placed it on her finger. She'd barely had a chance to take another look at it before he pulled her in his arms for a kiss sealing their fate as husband and wife even before they actually said their I do's.

Victoria went willingly into his arms and poured as much into the kiss as she was receiving. She would never again do anything that kept her from getting what she deserved and at this moment, she deserved to love and be loved by the man who turned out to be the man of her dreams.

"I don't know how I'm going to explain this to my family. Just recently they were celebrating my engagement to Turner and now I'm engaged to someone they've never even heard me mention. I need to write a book about my life because I'm sure this unbelievable story would be a hit," she said.

Tyrone laughed so hard he almost choked.

"My life hasn't been as dramatic as yours has been lately, but I can guarantee you, I have a grandmother who will at first be shocked and then immediately ecstatic hearing that I'm getting married. I think she believed it would never happen for me."

Victoria leaned into him, feeling perfect in his arms.

"What will you tell the group of single ladies who I'm sure won't believe that you're turning in your player's card to settle down with one woman."

"I'm less concerned about them than I am about how to help you deal with your family. Do they even know the circumstances around your engagement to Turner?"

"No they don't. All they know is that the engagement was called off, but I haven't had a chance to really talk to them because right after Turner and I broke things off, I got a flight out to come and talk to you. I was planning to talk to my family when I arrived and time got away from me. I need to sit down and talk to my family in person and explain everything."

"I'm going to come with you."

Victoria was shocked that he'd want to do that.

"I can't ask you to do that," she admitted.

"You're not asking Victoria, I'm offering. I love you and I want your family to know that. I want to be able to meet your dad and let him know that he can trust that I will never hurt you and that I will always take care of you. After everything that has taken place, I think they are going to need to know that this engagement is not fake and neither is my love for you."

Victoria smiled as her heart swelled with even more love for him.

"You are the perfect man for me. You're the kind of man fantasies are made of and you're all mine."

"Yes, I'm all yours. What do you think Turner will say?" he asked.

"He already knows we're together. That was him that called early this morning asking how things went. He got the gist when I rushed him off of the phone. He's happy that you and I were able to work things out. He and the woman he's been seeing are planning to get married and I'm glad because he and I both have found our love for a life time."

"We are a perfect combination," Tyrone said before kissing her with the promise of forever.

"After we talk to your family, I think I'm going to fly my grandmother here for a visit and introduce you to her. I know you need to get back to work, but when can we plan for you to make another trip here so that you can meet her. Let me also warn you that you may also end up meeting my mother."

Victoria was happy to hear that Tyrone's heart had softened when it came to his mother. He'd told her of his struggles to get over her leaving him.

"Baby, I'm ready to meet everyone who is important to you and even though you haven't exactly made amends with your mother, I'm happy to meet her as well. If she hadn't given birth to you, I wouldn't be here with you right now."

Tyrone leaned back on his chair and pulled Victoria on to his lap.

"I know we have a lot of details to work out when it comes to the wedding and where we'll live, but tonight, I want to love you and tune out everything else except you and me."

He pulled her to him and planted soft kisses on her face as he slowly began unbuttoning her blouse.

"I'm already planning on giving my notice and hightailing it back to Atlanta as soon as I can make that happen. I love you and I don't want to have a long distance relationship and where you are is where I want to be."

Tyrone smiled. He was hoping they could resolve the living situation soon. He wasn't sure he would be able to handle to many nights of being without her and knew that he'd be using a lot of frequent flyer miles to go back and forth between Atlanta and Boston to see her as often as possible.

"That sounds like music to my ears. Right now though, I'm done talking."

Victoria was on the same page. Talking was overrated when clearly they could be doing something much more interesting and satisfying. She reached down to help him finish undressing her and as she reached for the remote to turn off the television removing all distractions, she reveled in the touch and feel of the man she loved and thanked her lucky stars that nothing could keep her from her perfect love.

Epilogue

Tyrone stood at the altar along with Duron and Mike as his groomsmen, as he watched Victoria walk down the aisle on her father's arm. All of her family had come to Atlanta for the wedding. They'd decided to have the wedding in Atlanta instead of Washington where she was from or Boston where she'd lived for the past five years. She loved Atlanta especially after happily moving in with Tyrone seven months ago, leaving her job in Boston after applying for and landing a job in the Atlanta area. The job came through quicker than she and Tyrone had anticipated, but they went with it. Victoria easily sold her house and packed up her things for her move and never looked back.

Tyrone was excited that he'd hit it off great when he finally got the chance to meet her family. Her parents were a little leery at first, not knowing how to accept a second engagement from Victoria in such a short period of time. Once Turner and then Victoria had finally cleared that whole matter of their fake engagement up, her family had warmed to him, realizing his love for Victoria was real.

This was the happiest day of his life. He looked around

at all the guests who had arrived to celebrate the day with them.

His grandmother had flown in from Texas over a week ago and he loved that she had enjoyed a great time, especially with Duron's mother as they were becoming great friends. His grandmother was most thankful for the love and support Duron's family had always shown him. It was because of them that Tyrone never felt like he didn't have anyone since he lived so far away from her.

He also noticed Duron's family sitting on the front row. Duron's father was holding both of Duron and Taija's kids on his lap, one in each arm while Ms. Barbara held Mike and Loren's little boy Chase who had been born without complications. Their family was growing quickly.

Tyrone couldn't wait to start a family with Victoria, something they'd talked about extensively. They both wanted children right away. Tyrone admitted to her how lonely he'd felt growing up and knew that he was looking forward to filling their house with as many children as she wanted to have. He also wanted his grandmother to have a chance to see and love on her grandchildren. She had no health issues, but he knew that she couldn't wait to spoil any children they'd have.

Loren and Taija both stood on the opposite side of the aisle as bridesmaids looking beautiful.

As Victoria and her dad made their way to him, he never knew a woman could be as beautiful as Victoria as she walked hand in hand with him down the aisle in a Vera Wang gown made just for her.

Just as Victoria reached him and her father finally placed her hand in his, Tyrone took one last look at the crowd and smiled back at his mother who was happily enjoying the wedding. Over the months that had passed, he had developed a good rapport with her and they were working on getting closer. It was Victoria's idea to invite JoAnn, who he recently started calling mother, to the wedding. She didn't want to go into their marriage with any baggage and it was important to her that everyone who meant anything to them was present as they began their life together. She also wanted any children they had to have grandparents on both sides. Tyrone tried hard to let the past stay in the past.

When his mother asked him if he wanted to know who his father was, Tyrone declined the information. He figured after all these years, the man didn't want to have anything to do with them so he'd leave it that way. Maybe one day in the future he would be able to handle that information. For now, he was still learning how to have a mother in his life.

He and Victoria had prepared their own vows. They wanted the words they spoke to have extra meaning. After they said them, bringing tears to the eyes of almost everyone in attendance, the ministered declared them husband and wife. Before the words were out of the minister's mouth, Tyrone had already taken Victoria in his arms and kissed her, not letting up even though they had a room full of guests watching. When everyone clapped thinking Tyrone would turn her loose, they stopped when they realized he wasn't thinking about anyone else in the room, but his new wife.

"Ty," Duron leaned over and said. "Get a room, man. We're hungry."

Everyone laughed. Even Tyrone had to let go of Victoria's lips and laugh at himself. He'd waited what seemed an eternity to make Victoria his wife. Clearly he'd gotten carried away.

As they turned to be presented to everyone as Mr. and Mrs. Tyrone Davis, Tyrone saw Turner and his wife Cecily had entered the wedding and sat in the rear. Since the moment everything had been worked out, he and Victoria and Cecily and Turner had become great friends. He and Victoria flew to Washington to attend the wedding of the year when Turner and Cecily exchanged vows in a ceremony held on the grounds of the mansion he and Cecily would soon occupy. Tyrone's firm was also under contract to modernize that structure as well.

The reception was in full swing when Tyrone made an announcement.

"I want to thank everyone on behalf of Victoria and I for sharing in this day with us. Many of you who know me know of my fascination with cars. What some of you may not know is that Victoria has the same fascination. She once told me about this little white, vintage sports car that she'd admired as a child. She even had a picture of it. Well thanks to her parents, I was able to track down one of those cars and had it restored just for my wife."

Tyrone heard the room break out into claps and cheers. He saw that Victoria was bouncing up and down like a child with excitement when she realized he'd just said he'd bought her the car of her dreams.

"Where is it?" she shouted, not being able to contain her joy.

Tyrone loved his woman. She never ceased to amaze him.

"If everyone would join us outside for a moment, I'd like you all to meet the latest addition to our family of cars."

Before anyone else could move, Victoria took Tyrone by the hand after planting a kiss of thank you on his lips and headed in the direction of her car. Her eyes lit up like a Christmas tree when she saw the small white car sitting out front with a white bow on the back with a 'Just Married' sign underneath with tin cans that would drag when they drove away.

This was the best gift Victoria ever received besides the gift of love from the man of her dreams.

Victoria got behind the wheel of her new car just for a moment to see how it would feel. Her husband wanted to kick off their new life together in a big way by having this little baby restored just for her. She couldn't wait to get it on the open road and really open it up. This man of hers was truly her dream man. He understood her in a way that people who had known her since birth still couldn't figure out.

She'd had a love for cars since she was a child and this wedding gift to her was as perfect for her as any gift could ever be for anyone.

The wedding party and most of she and Tyrone's family and friends came outside to check out the car as well. She heard all of the *oohs* and *aahs* and could match their sentiment because it was a beauty. She didn't want to take away from the time spent enjoying the reception, so after a few more minutes she gathered up her dress as Tyrone, who helped her get in the car, stood by her to help her get out. She was about to close the car door when a flash of someone running past her caught her eye. It took Victoria a minute to realize that flash was Brian, Duron's brother. He was in a rush to get to his car and she hoped everything was okay.

"Baby, is Brian okay? Everything okay? He looks like he's running off to an emergency of some type?" Victoria asked as they closed the car door and headed back inside behind their guests to continue with the party. Tyrone looked to where Brian jumped in his car and after he barely had a chance to put the key in the ignition, the car sped off at a fast pace. Tyrone knew where he was headed. He just hoped things worked out for him. Right now all he wanted to think about was his beautiful wife.

~~

Brian made it to the airport and was about to board the private flight his brother Duron had secured for him when his cell phone rang. It was Duron.

"What's up Duron?"

"Hey bro, it's Jake and I both on the line. I patched him in before calling you. We wanted to check on you before you got too far. You shot out of the reception quick and we wanted to be sure you made it to the airport safely," Duron said.

"Yeah, I'm good. I'm just anxious to get to Baltimore and find out why Sherry has kept my daughter from me. It doesn't matter how our relationship ended, I had a right to know about my daughter," Brian shouted in anger through the phone. He knew his brothers didn't mind. They had been each other's sounding board since they were young children.

The private detective that Duron hired for him had done the job he was hired to do and had located Sherry and brought back the information he needed about his daughter. He was not only anxious, but he was also angry, something his brothers knew. The detective had sent back pictures of the little girl who could be Loren's daughter as

Brian's friend claimed originally. There was no doubt the little girl was a Knight which gave him no doubt that she was his. His anger continually reached the boiling over point every time he thought about it. Clearly the last time he'd tried to reach out to her she had been pregnant and didn't let him know which meant that she deliberately kept him from his daughter. He would soon confront her and get some answers. Thankfully he was on a break from teaching and if need be, he would take a leave of absence from work to make sure Sherry understood he wasn't going anywhere until she understood that he planned to be a part of his daughter's life whether she liked it or not. He had no intention of walking away from his flesh and blood.

"Brian it's me Jake. Listen, I know you're upset, believe me we hear the anger, but you need to taper that off some before you get to Baltimore. For starters, no matter how much that little girl looks like our family, you have to handle this the right way. Don't go barging in on their lives making demands. You need to talk to Sherry with a level head and let her tell you that the little girl is yours and if she doesn't, I recommend you convince her to let you have a paternity test done. Again, you need to ask her for it and not demand it like I know you would do."

Brian paced back and forth with determined steps after Jake told him what equaled to letting Sherry control what happens. He had no plans to do that since she'd been controlling things all along.

"I don't need a paternity test because I know she's mine. You both saw the pictures. Would either of you question the paternity if it were you and you saw how much that little girl looked like you? The minute I saw her cute little face in those pictures I had no doubt she was mine. If she tries to deny it then yeah I will ask her for a test. If she denies that then I'll use legal means."

"Brian, are you sure you want to do this alone?" Duron asked. "Jake has offered to come along with you. You know I would if the twins were older," he added.

"No, I'm good. By the time the plane lands I promise to rethink my approach and handle this calmly, but right now I'm venting to the two of you, but I'm good. I appreciate the support. I'm getting signaled that we are about to take off. Thank you for the love and you know I appreciate the private plane, Duron. I owe you a big one for this."

"You'll never owe me for anything. I look forward to meeting my niece soon. Call if you need anything and remember I have some attorneys in Baltimore that I can connect you to if you need them. I don't want you to have to fight with Sherry, but we don't walk away from family and that little girl is our family."

"Thanks bro. I will call with an update."

"Brian, by the way, what's our niece's name?" Duron asked before they got disconnected.

Brian smiled with excitement thinking about his daughter.

"Her name is Sherice," he said before hanging up so that the plane could take off.

Brian took the time on the flight to remember back to a time when he was happier than he thought he could ever be. That was until the love of his life ended their relationship and turned his life upside down.

He had met Sherry at a football game, of all places. He thought he was the biggest football fan until he attended a game and sat next to her and realized she'd had him beat. She shouted at failed plays, hollered at referees who shouted bad plays and even screamed at cheerleaders who weren't showing enough excitement. He watched her throughout the game and by the time it was over, he was already in love.

He tried to engage her in conversation several times and his friends laughed at him when she didn't pay him any attention. He thought all was lost and that she wasn't interested until the game ended and she turned to him with her hand extended as if to shake it and introduced herself. She apologized for her rudeness during the game and explained that when football was on, she was completely focused on the game. He shook her hand, smiled and introduced himself.

The game had ended and everyone had left the stadium except the two of them. He and Sherry sat for over an hour talking and ended up going out to dinner and talked until the restaurant threw them out. After that day, they were inseparable. For months, she was his everything and he thought she'd felt the same way. He had even introduced her to his family and invited her to a few family functions.

Things were going great, or so he thought until one day she told him the relationship was over with no real explanation other than she felt like he'd betrayed her and she never wanted to see him again. He had no clue what happened and tried to get her to explain, but came up empty. She didn't give him any more of an explanation. He decided to let her cool off and when he went to visit her at her apartment in downtown Atlanta a week later, she'd already moved out without leaving a forwarding address. He knew her parents lived in Baltimore and reached out to them assuming she'd gone back home. Whatever had caused their breakup had been shared with her family because it was her father who told him that he thought it was best that Brian leave their daughter alone because he had hurt her enough. He didn't understand, but he abided by her father's wishes. His parents had taught him to be respectful and he had his graduation from graduate school to prepare for. Back then she wanted nothing to do with him and as much as he cared about her, he moved on not wanting to beg for a woman who no longer wanted him. She was a junior at Clark-Atlanta University and never returned the next semester. When he no longer heard from her he stopped trying to get answers on how she felt he had betrayed her, something he knew he had not done, but she wouldn't talk to him and explain what he had done that caused her to walk away from a relationship that he thought was on a path to something more permanent.

He was several years older than her, but age didn't matter to him and he thought it hadn't mattered to her. He couldn't imagine then or now what could have gone wrong and after she'd walked away from him without cause, he no longer wanted to know. The only thing that mattered to him was that they had a daughter together and Sherry had a lot of explaining to do about why she didn't tell him that Sherice existed. In a few hours, he planned to get answers and he wasn't leaving Baltimore until he did.

Brian looked out of the airplane window as the private jet descended for landing. For a split second, he questioned his decision to drop in on Sherry not knowing how she would receive his presence and if she would even allow him to see his daughter. He hoped things didn't turn into a blowout session, but he was determined to at least get some answers.

In the months that they had dated, he'd fallen in love

with her though he never told her. He loved where their relationship was and didn't want to pressure her into being in love if she wasn't ready on her own and then she blindsided him by breaking up with him and leaving. He could have found her earlier and he would have if he had known about Sherice. Brian smiled again when he thought of the beautiful little girl in the pictures he'd seen of her. She appeared to be a happy little girl and he was glad to know that Sherry had not married though she was involved with a man and the thought of that didn't sit well with him. Sherry could be involved with anyone she chose to, but he had issues if the man was a father figure in his daughter's life. That he would not settle for. He was here and he was here to stay and be a father to his daughter, not caring if Sherry liked it or not.

After his flight landed and he made his way through the airport to pick up his rental, his level of excitement increased at the thought of seeing Sherry again and finally laying eyes on his little girl. He decided to not waste time checking into his hotel which was not far from the airport. It had been a long time since he'd last seen Sherry and he was anticipating the feeling of finally setting eyes on his little girl.

Using the GPS in the car, he quickly made his way through traffic and now found himself sitting outside of her parent's house contemplating how to approach them without being thrown out before he even said a word. It was now or never he decided.

Brian was about to exit the car to ring the bell when he noticed Sherry coming out of the house with the cutest little girl with the longest, thickest and bounciest braids held together by big pink and white ribbons. They must have been on their way to something fun because even at her little size, she was pulling her mother along as if she was in a hurry. Brian was amazed at how much Sherice not only looked like his sister Loren, but she also favored his niece Lyric. She was dressed in a denim jumper, covering a pink and white blouse and little pink and white tennis. She was beautiful and no doubt, his.

He was so overwhelmed with emotion upon seeing the Sherice he didn't care if Sherry wanted to see him or not. He wasn't leaving until they talked.

He exited his car and followed them to the playground across the street from the house. He approached and cleared his throat so that he didn't startle as he walked up behind Sherry after she placed Sherice in a swing an began pushing her.

"Hello Sherry," he said softly from behind her.

There was no need for her to turn around for him to know that she recognized his voice. He watched as her back stiffened and she ceased pushing their daughter on the swing.

Sherry didn't turn around, but Sherice looked around at the mysterious man who spoke and his heart melted when her hazel colored eyes stared back at him. She had the same eyes as Duron and Loren. Sherice was all Knight and there was no denying it and in the back of his mind, he dared Sherry to even try it.

Now that Sherice had noticed him, there was no way Sherry was going to be able to ignore his presence. He watched her turn, as if in slow motion until she was standing face to face with him. Brian's first thought was that she was just as beautiful now as she had been almost three years ago since he's last seen her.

He watched as she plastered what looked like a fake smile on her face and he assumed it was for the sake of Sherice as not to startle her.

"Brian, what are you doing here," she said, looking around suspicious like as if she was looking for someone else to show up.

"I came to Baltimore to talk to you," he said.

"Talk about what?" she replied.

"Mommy, push," Sherice said, drawing Brian's attention.

"Okay baby, mommy's pushing."

"That's a beautiful little girl you have," Brian said.

Sherry looked at him, realizing he had figured it out, but she didn't respond.

"I'm assuming the reason you are here in Baltimore is because you somehow found out about her after all this time."

"Were you going to tell me about her?"

"Tell you what, Brian?"

"Sherry, I don't even have to ask you for a blood test. Look at her. I know you know my sister Loren and she looks exactly like Loren did as a little girl and could pass as her daughter right now. Are you going to tell me she's not mine?" he asked quietly not sure how much his daughter would pick up on.

"Mommy, push!" Sherice shouted impatiently at the non-moving swing.

Sherry didn't realize that she'd stopped pushing the swing. She was trying to contain her surprise at seeing Brian and knowing that he also knew about Sherice.

She started pushing the swing again.

"I can't do this with you right now Brian," she said

looking around to see if anyone was watching them.

"I came a long way to see you and her and I'm not going away so we can talk now or we can do this later, but know that I'm not leaving Baltimore until we talk and I don't care how long it takes."

"Smile when you talk to me. Sherice is a very bright little girl and she will sense the tension. I don't want her frightened."

Without giving it a second thought, Brian plastered a smile on his face and the smile turned genuine when Sherice smiled back at him.

"Thank you," Sherry said, happy that he was thinking about Sherice and that he didn't want to upset her.

"I'm not here to make waves in your life Sherry. I would have left you alone as you asked me to years ago if it hadn't been for the fact that you have my daughter and I knew nothing about her. I'm going to keep smiling while I ask you again. Are you going to tell me that she's not mine?"

Sherry hesitated knowing that there was no way she'd be able to honestly deny Sherice was his. Everyday her daughter looked more and more like him and any denial would be useless.

"No Brian, I'm not going to tell you that."

She turned around while pushing her daughter on the swing and looked Brian in the eyes as her features softened.

"This is your daughter, Brian. I'd like you to meet Sherice Briana Knight."

Brian looked from Sherry to the little girl who was oblivious to what was going on around her because she was enjoying the swing. She only focused on being on the swing and paid no attention to them as any fight he had come prepared to have dissipated. Sherry confirmed what he already knew which was that he was a father of a beautiful little girl.

Before he could say anything, Sherry stopped whatever he was about to say.

"Before you go all into father mode and start making demands, this is my life and my daughter and I don't want or need anything from you so you can turn around and go back home Brian because you're not welcomed here," she said with anger that she was trying to hide from Sherice.

He didn't want to upset the little girl either so he smiled even though he was angry.

"Get use to me being here Sherry because like I already told you, I'm not leaving here without my daughter knowing who I am or without you and I talking about visitation and joint custody. You've selfishly kept me from my daughter long enough and that ends today. I'll let you decide whether we do this the hard way or the easy way, but now that I know she exists, I'm about to become a permanent fixture in your life so get used to it. I let you walk out of my life years ago without any kind of explanation of what I did that sent you away, but I won't let you keep my daughter from me. I've already missed two years of her life and I'm not missing anymore. The only question I have for you is do we tell her together that I'm her father or shall I do that on my own? I'm going to continue smiling so that Sherice is not frightened, but I want you to know that I will use any means at my disposal to make sure you don't keep her from me anymore."

Look for Brian and Sherry's in **Love at Last**, coming

soon.

What was Brian Knight to do when the woman whom he had fallen in love with told him she didn't want to see him again. She didn't give him any reason or explanation. She just left him and never looked back.

Sherry Braxton wasn't happy to see Brian Knight appear out of nowhere wanting to claim her daughter as his and trying to insert himself as a part of their lives whether she wanted him to or not.

Brian had watched both of his brothers find women that made them happy and they now lived happy lives as husbands and fathers. He couldn't find that happiness because he'd never gotten over the one that got away, Sherry.

Now that he was a part of her life once again, he had no plans of letting her get away, no matter how hard she pushed him away. For the sake of his daughter, he was in their lives to stay.

Make sure you get your copy of **Bachelor Not For Sale**, Duron & Taija's story and **A Designed Affair**, Mike & Loren's Story available now in paperback and hardcopy on the author's website at www.cherylbarton.net

Bachelor Not For Sale
Duron & Taija's story

Even self-proclaimed "bachelors for life" meet that one woman that makes them want to slow down and second guess bachelorhood. After suffering through the heartache of what he thought was true love, Duron Knight meets and becomes enchanted with bombshell Taija Charles. Taija has heard a lot about Duron and all of her body senses are on overdrive when she meets the handsome bachelor face to face. As the sparks fly, Taija plans to show Duron how she can help him mend his broken heart with real love and the right amount of lust.

A Designed Affair
Loren & Mike's story

In the follow-up to "Bachelor Not For Sale", Loren Knight has been engaging in a secret love affair with her brother Duron's best friend and business partner, Michael Bailey. He is everything she could want and more in a man, but she believes the risk is too great for any type of relationship with him beyond the bedroom door. Michael Bailey has been fighting his attraction to Loren for years. He has stayed away from her out of respect for his best friend and business partner. Now that he and Loren have finally given into passion that they both have been craving, can Michael convince Loren that what they share is well worth the risk?

Other books by Author Cheryl Barton

AMOROUS OCCUPATIONS: THE ARTIST

Zora Michaels, a local Boston artist spends all of her time working and focused on her next achievement. The war in Iraq took the life of the one man who loved her and her bohemian, artsy lifestyle. She no longer wants love. She only wants to paint. Micah Prentiss had the perfect life, a beautiful wife, a baby about to come into the world, when that world changed with her sudden passing during child-birth. The only love he ever wanted to experience again was the love he had for his child until the passion he found in a painting reminded him of what true love is all about. Come discover a second chance at love that will last forever!!

AMOROUS OCCUPATIONS: THE BOOKKEEPER

FBI agent Karen Jacobs is finally getting her first undercover assignment. Her cover assignment as a bookkeeper is an easy transition for her with her background in finance. Business owner Thomas Atwater couldn't believe his eyes when he saw the love of his life walk into the restaurant where he was having lunch. Seeing her sparked feelings he thought had died long ago when she walked out on him. Karen, discovering the object of the investigation is Thomas, the one and only man she ever truly loved, has to find a way to do her job while fighting feelings for him that she thought she had buried years ago.

AMOROUS OCCUPATIONS: THE CHEF

Chef Charles Watts, owner of "Watt You Say?", the most popular restaurant in Chicago, is looking to expand his restaurant by purchasing the building next door. His one obstacle is trying to convince his bombshell neighbor, Jennifer Taylor, to move her bakery to another location. Her late night backing and his late night cooking lead to some fiery early morning rendezvous.

ABOUT THE AUTHOR

Cheryl Barton lives in Maryland and in her spare time she enjoys reading, writing, spending time with her family, line dancing and eating Maryland steamed crabs.

Visit her website at http://www.cherylbarton.net and be sure to leave her a comment. You can connect with her on Twitter @mscbarton and on Facebook at Author Cheryl Barton.

Happy Reading☺